People think be good and you go to heaven,

Bad you go to hell

That's kind of true,

But the stories always miss a step

See hell isn't a destination,

It's the journey before heaven

**And not everyone makes it**

D1428850

# Chapter 1

## Ne Obliviscaris

"Fuck off Lewis I'm sleeping, go away",
"No fuck off its time for school, come on come on", It's the same each morning I have to wake up to this little voice in my ear and small hands shaking my arm as I cower into my pillow at 7am. I can hear my little brother Lewis running off down the stairs, like he always does excited for school and my only thoughts are why doesn't he just let me sleep? What was I dreaming about?
I hate mornings, if I had my way it would be 1pm earliest and seriously school, 8 hours of teachers telling us the curriculum is fucked up but they have to use it anyway. I can't think of many things I've learnt over the years, not sure how my knowledge of photosynthesis is going to help or how being graded on my third year art clock I made three nights before it was due is going to prepare me for life, did get a B for it though. The only reason to go to school is to see my mates, P.E. and Mia Rose, puberty you winner. Shame she doesn't see me the same way with my good looks and charming personality. I'm 14 years old, not hugely built but I can hold my own in a fight and there are some signs of an ab or two. I have short mousy brown hair, enough to spike but not enough to Jedward my look. Blue eyes no facial hair yet and sadly a face like the dark side of the moon, there is just not enough Clearasil to remedy the situation. My room is a collection of movie posters, games consoles (inc an original NES not that anyone is asking) and what looks like an addiction to lynx Africa after a succession of repetitive Christmas and birthday presents. Then there's waking up every morning with

this thing staring at the ceiling, the human body is weird, only one thing for it I suppose.

"RYAN! Downstairs your breakfast is out and you have 15 minutes till the bus gets here, get your arse in gear before my foot needs to give it a kick start!" Always a sweet charmer my mum never mixes her words, she has one of those voices that never requires a megaphone and can send most adults into a frenzied P.T.S.D. of their child hood scalding's just by counting down. I suppose the day has to start somewhere, at least it's my birthday next week and dad says it's an important one. We have even got my Grandad coming up from York, which doesn't happen often. He wasn't from York originally, he actually came from Ireland, moved to west coast of Scotland and then south. He always comes up on the weekend of our birthdays which means a guaranteed 50 quid. Destiny (the game) comes out soon, it's been a tough month, but home-work all done and the 6 months report card aced (they don't need the truth). I'm set to play my Xbox till the neighbours complain about the smell.

"Strength of the pack is the wolf; Strength of the wolf is the pack" gives me Goosebumps every time.

I live with my mum, dad and three brothers in a small Fort town called Brathaidh east of Carlisle, don't bother trying to find it on the map, apparently we are so insignificant we're barely worth the dot, the town at least does have its appeal. It used to be a Great Fort held by some Duke who's greatest claim was that it was never breached. I'm guessing that was because it was never found, but still a fairly big boast. Most of our parents in the area work in the same office-based businesses dealing with government contracts and stuff like that. The Fort is made up of two walls of solid sandstone, the inner wall is a large square with towers in all four corners and all the town shops etc are located within and around the town statue in the middle. The inner fort is surrounded by a shallow moat that was once fairly deep but drained for safety reasons after some teenagers nearly lost their lives. Out with the central wall and moat, is a huge hexagonal wall around 10ft thick also with towers on all points. On the south side is the main entrance, a huge steel and ebony wood gate with intricate Celtic designs that is never closed. The Fort has a main bridge leading from the gate to the main road that goes across the moat. The bridge is a beautiful sand and lime stone carved structure that replaced the old draw bridge over 100 years ago, it is big enough for cars to pass either side and path ways for pedestrians. A couple of decades ago, two extra roads slightly smaller were built into the east and west walls intersecting at the town square, this created a sort of round-about in the centre. Outside of the Fort on the North-west side is the Town Park, a small play area with swings and slide built around the towns Great Oak said to be hundreds of years old and climbed by many generations. On the south west side is the town's cathedral, an old relic of the Templars but used mainly as the town hall. Further down the road is the local lake popular with fishermen and wildlife enthusiasts. On the eastern side of town is the town's residents, a selection of houses and schemes that have built up over the years of population growth. Slightly south east is the local schools, Brathaidh Primary and Brathaidh Academy. They were separate but with expansion, everything from nursery to high school became one large complex. Most of the area outside of town limits is dense forests with one main route south and a route west to Carlisle. I would have loved to have seen the place during its military occupation, the tower filled with guards and the functioning draw bridge. The local council still goes a long way to keep the battlements and main gate in good form I guess as a way to try keep up some level of tourism.

My chaotic family is made up of four boys, what were they thinking right? Worst of all we are two sets of twins, which is apparently very common in our family. My twin is James he's not identical just born on the same day two hours earlier, you'd think it was 2 years the way he was sometimes. He likes cars more than computer games and has a real soft spot for old VW Beetles, he could change a tyre by the age of ten (with a bit of help) and dad always encouraged him to try see what else he could fix. We had plenty of space in our garage so dad got a scrapper beetle from a local dealer and James has spent every second he can trying to learn more about it and fix it up. He is always covered in oil if he can manage it, megalomaniac aside he is however fiercely loyal and good company when mums on the war path, he always has my back. The two youngest are 4 years old, identical and I swear serve no other purpose than to torment me. Lewis and Liam or as I like to call them thing one and thing two, Liam did try for chocolate thunder but I wasn't budging not matter how much the cat in the hat said so. They spend most of their time getting into spaces they shouldn't for reasons best known only to themselves, we once had to retrieve them from a local burn because they were climbing fences and toppled into the water. Mum is as I said is very loud and doesn't need a speakerphone to let the neighbourhood know that dinner is ready, she always looks after us and her hugs are the best. Mum is 5ft tall, a little plump and grey at the tips. She might not look it but I wouldn't take her in a fight, in her youth she put a guy through reinforced glass just for getting on her last nerve. Sometimes I think even dad is scared of her when she's pissed off and he rarely flinches. She's always good for a laugh, barely has any eyebrows because she lost them during several flame related incidents, note to self don't try to blow out a methylated spirit fondue set, she looked permanently surprise for weeks which led to no end of torment from us. My dad works in an office down town but the way he goes on you would think it was the military, he has always got us exercising at the weekends, doing track and teaching us martial arts. He even takes us shooting sometimes which always leads to competitions except when grandad comes, he always wins. Dad never really speaks about his work and sometimes is very quiet when he comes home like there was a report he just couldn't handle or something, mum says it's not polite to ask him as its important work and we will find out one day. We used to pretend he was a secret agent and when he went to work is was code for I'm off to stop Goldfinger or some villain. That was until we saw him trying to navigate his way around Scarborough on a family holiday; right then we ruled it out. James bond would never have stopped at traffic lights and lost his shit over directions. He did train us how to fight really well something he was quite passionate about it, James even considered going into a mixed martial arts tournaments but got a girlfriend three days before sign up and suddenly the thought of being anywhere else went away. If you believe him so did his second base virginity but he gets sketchy when anyone asks for specifics, even after they broke up.

Anyway now for the hard trudge that is school, sometimes I feel like if there was a choice between going to school or grabbing a huge dog turd and clapping, I would give a riotous round of applause.

Its first period and I have computing class, not a terrible way to start the day and teacher generally leaves us to it. This usu-ally means half the class is trying to find out which house the sorting hat will put them in on Pottermore and the other half trying to guess the admin password so they can visit skin sites. My mate Simon and I know the password, but we're smart enough to wait until out of the teacher's sight to be using it and not pass it around so that it gets changed. Simon is one of my partners in crime (as the teachers like to say) and so is Brian, the bro-mance between those two would raise eye-brows if not for how quickly they both pause for a set of Double Ds. They both came over from America and moved into the town at the beginning of 1st year. They have been plaguing the school with their nonsense ever since, which was an instant hit in my books. Simon has dark short hair and a wiry frame. He is a really fast runner, quick witted and loves terrible dad jokes. Brian is Afri-can American, very broad shouldered for his age and definitely the muscles of the group. He is quieter than Simon but no less devious, has a wicked sense of humour when he is in his comfort zone. Their latest trick is hiding a cheap phone they purchased, in random spots around the class and ringing it to wind up the teacher. One teacher stormed out screaming to shut the phone off because he couldn't find it, I was sure they were going to get caught that time but those two always have an alibi ready.

The rest of my year is generally the typical mix of go-getters, slackers, "secret" smokers and know it all's. Then there's Mia, Auburn hair couple of freckles, blue eyes and dimples when she smiles. It's safe to say I'm hooked or as Simon once said about our P.E teacher

"I would drag my balls over broken glass to smell her socks". I watched her break the nose on a 6<sup>th</sup> year that grabbed her ass a week ago, I think she could give James a run for his money with that right hook of hers. I would take it just to get her attention.

"Hey dude have you got the game pre-ordered yet? Me and Brian are heading along to HMV after school to get ours booked" Simon smiled wide eyed at me and I had my mother's voice in my head "Brian and I" she never misses an opportunity to correct me. "He's going the Titan and I'm going the Hunter, if you go the Warlock we will have a mental fire team" I put my pre-order request in a month ago and Warlock was already my plan but nice to see it works out any way.

"Yeah man, on it like a fat kid on cake. Did you go for the legen..." what was that? I paused "Get the what?" Brian asked staring me out. It took me a second to recover

"what? The legendary pack? You know you get the season pass expansions and that?"

Simon scoffs

"mate its 70 quid, it can bugger off, get base game for now see if it's any good". Shit 70 quid, my grandad only gives me 50, I hope someone else is feeling generous this year. What was that thing that flicked passed the window? It looked like a man with mouse blonde hair but... smokier and white pupils... odd. Maybe I should lay off the energy drinks, I started getting the shakes the other day after two cans and I really need to pee a lot too.

One Week Later

Finally, it's my birthday and as an added bonus it's the weekend and that means I'll be in the store to collect my order by 11 and gaming by 12. Maybe if my Grandad is feeling extra generous I might even get some munch for the day and really hibernate. Listening closely I can hear the low rumble of an engine in the distance and speak of the devil, there's his car pulling into the drive. I have never seen a man so proud of a Volvo estate car, don't get me wrong the thing is a tank. He took on the neighbour's wall with it once and it didn't so much as dent his bumper. At least we can see where James gets his love of cars from, grandad has shown James a few things over the years and tools to use, but James has read his Haynes manual so thoroughly there were few things he couldn't do or tell you. Ever since I saw him on Game of Thrones, Grandad always reminded me of Sir Davos. The voice, the disposition and the sideways grin were all very convincing. I started calling him the onion knight but he got pissed off so much that I kept it to myself, mostly.

"Grandad!!" shouted the evil minions in unison and on cue as always. I head downstairs to the front door to greet Grandad, James shuffles in next to me in the hallway

"what you gonna do with yours this year? I've got my eyes on a new spanner set" no surprise there, 15 years old and sounds like grandad "Xbox game bro, you know me" Grandad hands the youngest two a bag of sweets and some kids magazines

"here you go boys enjoy" Dad gestures to the two of us "come in the living room you two, Lewis and Liam take your sweets upstairs to your room" This is different, usually gifts are a family event. We have to wait until everyone gathers round and the customary caterpillar cake for each of us is presented along with our gift "come on boys we haven't got all day come on in dad, you've remembered to bring them haven't you?" Grandad stands at his full height and squares up with Dad

"I didn't forget on your birthday and definitely wouldn't forget on theirs". I can see where Dad got his bearings from, when Grandad gets fired up he still looks like he can put up a hell of a fight, Dad says his nickname was Popps in the yard and everyone looked up to him or got out of his way.

"Right you two, hands out" James and I stand side by side with our hands out, waiting for that wonderful white envelope containing either a comical card from dad and grandad or a soppy card from mum and 5 wonderful £10 notes. But this time grandad hands us each a polished wooden box about the size of a book, which we weren't expecting, or hoping for.

"What's this?" I said trying not to sound as disappointed as I was "it's a boxed up dog turd" grandad says with a big smirk on his face "Open it and you'll find out you daft sod" The box was black wood with silver hinges. I looked at the markings on the box, silver symbols lined the outer edges and I opened the box and looked inside. It was a silver shield like a large broach emblazoned with a Boar's head and the words "Ne Obliviscaris" across the top. I stare trying to mouth out the words on the shield like I'm watching the magic pencil

"It means Forget not" I looked up at my dad confused "that's what it means its Gaelic, it's our family motto and sigil, though a bit different to the original design".

"Uhh Thanks" James and I say in unison trying to pull a smile on our faces. Grandad starts to chuckle

"Hahaha you boys have no idea what this means and what's instore for you both". He was right. We have no idea why anyone would give this as a birthday gift over 50 quid and even less of an idea as to why we had to make such an evet of it. That's parents I guess and it was kind of cool I suppose. It wasn't a, defend the planet from aliens with cool weapons and super powers kind of cool, but it looked ok and the box was nice.

# Chapter 2

## *The Splintered Sword*

"So what... does all this mean exactly?" I ask curiously and still holding the box as though there was a hole in the bottom.

"what it means" said grandad swivelling around to me

"is that today you both can begin training at the Office. Just like I did and just like your father did when we were your age, for the family business" This wasn't making me feel better and the face that James pulled I thought the box was about to get thrown out the window

"The family business?" I burst out

"dad works in an office, I don't want to train to shovel papers". Dad stepped forward but got interrupted by Grandad

"your father doesn't push papers and hasn't sat at a desk since I trained him to hold a sword, But standing in here isn't going to explain anything we must go to the Office immediately or we are going to be late and make sure to bring those shields with you". This was not how I planned the day to go but before we knew it James and I were being herded into the car. Liam and Lewis were scrambling to come with us but dad sent them back inside the house to see mum. This just added to the weirdness and they were not impressed by not being able to come.

We headed into town driving round the statue of the duke before pulled up in the car park outside our local pub. It was different to most of the other buildings as it was the only one actually built into the fortress wall on the north side with its own battlements and large entrance. It also had the words karaoke every Tuesday on a cheap banner over the door. It was a cool place and good food. James and I always tried to get dad to let us get a drink here and I looked over almost gleefully thinking he would today

"dad this is the pub, not that I'm complaining but Mum will kill you if she finds out" says James mockingly, dad gives a wee chuckle

"yeah keep dreaming boys got a few years yet" The Red lion, one of the most generic bar names since ever, dad always loved the cliché of going nearly anywhere in the world and finding one. We get out the car and start walking in, Grandad pipes up walking in behind us

"Haha people always think, go to church the house of the lord, get a word with God" grandad sniggers "this is the real route to the heavens boys just you wait and see" dad interrupts him

"dad keep it down". We stepped into the bar area and I looked around. The room bore the aroma of many a poured pint and was decorated with an old sort of Viking/Celt like feel using horn shaped lamps, wooden tables and benches with Celtic designs carved all around. Dad nodded to the man behind the counter who was polishing bottles of fine Malt Whisky. "Morning Peter, Richard, these the new recruits?" said the barman, dad turns to us "yup, it's time they got the grand tour. We walked round the bar to the back rooms where the toilets, yard and bar offices were. I'm not going to lie if Dad has taken us all the way back here to tap on a stone wall for a laugh, I will swing for him

"just through here boys" Dad moves down a corridor to a door marked private, I looked up at the plaque above the door and read aloud

"The Path to Redemption" dad looks at me "Yup, look on the back of your shield", I looked on the back where a bunch of weird symbols had started lightly glowing

"those symbols are the keys to Purgatory you must keep them safe and on you at all times, you'll see" He turns around, places his hand on the door said out loud "Ne Obliviscaris" the door ahead made a "ting" noise and a white light shimmered briefly around the edge. The strange symbols appeared on the door glowing like the ones on the shield and the whole door glowed slightly

"Welcome boys, to the office" dad pushed the door ahead open and walked forward. I walked in behind him and blinked as my eyes adjusted from the dark corridor to reveal a bright massive expanse of fine polished steel, dark marble work tops and ebony flooring as far as they eye could see. There were stairs leading to upper levels wrapped around what looked like the largest reception desk I have ever seen, Seats in rows behind the desk seemed to go on for miles. On the left and right were more gates with parents and teenagers walking in with the same look of bemusement as my own. Looking around at the people walking past and working away, some people were in different designs of black and silver armour and cloaks walking in groups equipped with weapons. Others in military office garments were carrying clip boards and escorting people across the building. Then there were the "everyday" people that looked like they were glowing with a kind of faint aura, but wearing everyday clothes being guided places wearing lanyards around their necks. James was the first to pipe up

"either we've walked into the fucking Tardis or I missed something on the back of the pub" "hahaha strong language my boy save some for the field" laughed grandad

"Dr Who wishes his Tardis was this big, we are no longer in Brathaidh lads, this is purgatory the plain between plains" James looks over to dad who looks at us and starts walking backwards, puts his arms out grabbing the attention of other teenagers staring in wonder and says "Welcome to the British branch of the Purgatory Apparition Transit Heritage" I looked at my dad

"Seriously?" he turned round

"Yeah to be honest we think they were struggling to think up some way to use the word Path, it was a P.R. nightmare a few decades ago" I was still taking in the view as he said it "why does that matter?". He turned back to me "I son, am a Pathfinder, Major Peter Campbell of The British Division. Just like my father and like you and James are going to be, with no small amount of luck" The smile on his face didn't reveal if this was an elaborate hoax or not. James spoke up

"so what Path, are we looking for exactly? And I can't stress this enough, why?" The tannoy system bellowed overhead

"all new recruits please report to assembly hall for induction". Dad shuffles us along

"no time to explain boys you need to get a move on that announcement was for you". In the hall dad points out some chairs marked for us, he then grabs my shoulder

"Just remember if you think it's funny, keep it to yourself, chances are you'll regret saying it out loud" he pats my back and we move in.

We sat looking all around at faces holding the same level of awe as our own. Dad and Grandad were hanging back at the entrance talking with the other parents as we and the other new recruits shuffled about with eyes fixed on the podium across the room. A stern fluorescent white haired woman walked into the room from a door on the left. She strode in her black and silver military style uniform and made her way to the front podium. The room very quickly fell silent as she reached the microphone

"Welcome new recruits, to the Office. I am Commander Joanne Mcmail and I am in charge of this facility. Firstly I would like to welcome you all to the Office and thank your parents for their support. This is one of our largest induction years for some time with many new recruits around the world coming of age to join our ranks. Not everyone will be inducted today so bear with us as we organise everything to come. I know you are all finding out about all this today and there is a lot to explain and trust me when I say that all will become clear. What you may not realise is that many of you are all travelling in from different parts of the country Scotland, England, Wales and Ireland which is why you won't know many others sitting beside you. Your families as of today will be given authorisation to divulge information and classified knowledge about what we do here and why it is going to matter to the world that you are. Bringing you here today helps a lot of recruits come to grips with the scale of our operation, to witness the reality of it all and of course to receive your induction packs. Over the next few weeks and for the next 5 years you are going to begin training for one of the greatest honours any human can know, along with some of the greatest dangers. Not all of you will become a Pathfinder, the soldiers of our organisation. Some of you will join the Office clerical staff and help with operations that make everything we do both possible and efficient. Please know this, no matter what job you do here your contribution is vital for all humanity and you will be answering a calling you were born in to". James turns to me

"Anyone comes near me with a razor and says the word buzzcut they are getting drop kicked" I sniggered at this a little too loudly. The Commander on the podium shouted over

"And a special welcome to the Campbell twins" she announced, I could feel her eyes piercing through me "I'm sure given your lineage we can expect you two to be front of the class" I felt a lot of eyes look in our direction and felt my face turned red. "I thank you all for turning up today and I look forward to seeing you all at training in our academy. Now please get your schedule's locker keys and uniforms from the kiosk next to the front desk. Parents please proceed and let them know what they are in for". The speech was short and explained nothing. We were excused and went over to our dad who had a big grin on his face "I told you if you think it's funny keep it to yourself, that woman misses nothing".

"What did she mean our lineage?" dad looks at grandad and back at me

"I'll explain another time, for now I'll explain what you need to know today when we get home. We need to go the front desk and pick up your stuff. You boys will be happy to know you're only going to be in school part time from now on". At least some good has come from all this.

It was a quiet car journey home with no one really talking, I stared out of the car window loosing myself in thought over what I had just seen. We got home and Dad gestures us to the living room again "sit down and get comfy it's time to explain and it's not going to happen in five minutes". If there's one thing I didn't expect it was my mum to be sitting down with tears in her eyes as she looked at us.

"My boys are growing up so fast" she blubbers, runs over and hugs us tight and kisses us both on the cheek then sits back down, holding her trade mark red and white tea towel tight. "Right" dad shuts the door and sits down then begins to start as grandad finds his seat. "Heaven and Hell, you remember the Sunday school stuff right?" how could we forget a non-religious family attending Sunday school for giggles. I reckoned it was mum and dad trying to get us out the house for the afternoon. James says that's how Liam and Lewis came about, on a Sunday. I try not to think about it that's my parents.

"Well to a certain and very limited degree, it's true. We use modern names for a lot of things, but most cultures and religions have been clued onto its existence for many years and the people involved with its running, so to speak" Dad pauses so he can gather his thoughts, he can see that James and I are looking for a camera so we can play down any belief that this is all true, but we did go through a magic door-way not that long ago so I guess we both thought this warranted paying attention for five minutes.

"You see it's not as simple as be good you're going to heaven and bad you go to hell, you see ALL souls must pass through hell first. It used to be that some souls would just go to purgatory, never leave and just fade out of existence. Others would brave the hell scape to get a chance at what is called redemption. Very few ever made it and were often captured by the demons that guarded the plains. Some were tortured for all eternity, others were consumed to make the demons stronger, but the worst of mankind became abominations equal or more terrible than their crimes on earth. I can tell you Jack the Ripper made a hell of a mess when he got there, took many Pathfinder to take him down. You see some souls want to be captured; they wander off as though the demons are calling to them. Trying to do our job can get real difficult with these people so between them and demons we need to be very alert. I'm getting side tracked, basically great nasty creatures held in depths of hell capable of bad things. It is my job and was your Grandads job to escort souls to what is called redemption, great gates they must pass through where they get a chance at heaven, we reach them either passed or through the monsters that guard hell. Are you following me so far?" James seemed to catch on first

"Security detail for dead people?" Dad bobbles his head

"yeah kind of, it's dangerous, ridiculously dangerous which is why not everyone gets to become a Pathfinder, you also don't get to choose who you protect and who you don't" I frowned

"so guy murders kids and I have to save him and let him go to heaven?" Dad looks at me

"not save, guide. You see redemption isn't a guaranteed ticket to go to heaven or what even the next plain is, it's where souls will be tested and I suppose judged. By making sure they get to the gate, we can stop hell from overflowing or bigger creatures being let loose" beginning to comprehend I nod my head.

"Have you boys ever heard of a picture called, Dante's nine levels of hell?" I look at James who says

"the name rings a bell, think that guy Tom Hanks might have painted it right?" Dad sighs "Sounds familiar I guess" I said. Dad not so convinced

"it is a depiction from a famous poem by Dante Alighieri about him and his friend Virgil's trek through hell down the 9 levels of hell. The painting is actually quite interesting, worth a trip to a museum or even a google. Well back then people were a bit more black and white about what level they thought sinners had to be on and to be honest Dante was probably holding a bit of a grudge against people in some of his" dad paused for a second

"recollections, but it made for a good story" I looked at him

"recollections?" he looks at me

"yes he worked an office at the time and listened to the stories that Pathfinders took back from their adventures, they weren't

strictly accurate encounters of what is down there and he did step a toe into hell at one point, but he was definitely a paper man than a soldier. Anyway there are nine levels that we know of, with many gates in different locations and they are in a massive labyrinth of tunnels that we have to navigate, we can sometimes be in the tunnels for a couple of days but most trips are only hours. Depending on how heavy your sins were in life is what level you go to in hell; the Egyptians even mention the nine gates in their versions of death. There is a level 0 for the "pure" as they are referred, kids who have died and the very rare pure souled adults. Mother Teresa got a good send off from what I heard, the pure barely need escorted to their gate but we do it out of duty as small creatures still roam the top. Most adults have to go to level one or two. We all have regrets and life isn't perfect, levels 3 to 6 you can usually see some pretty guilty faces but they are generally harmless. I tell you tax fraud will catch up with you, many a politician gets down a few levels" he lets out a small chuckle at this. James speaks up before me
"so what sins get you to the different levels" Dad thinks for a second
"to be honest that answer isn't always clear, we don't have a case file telling us what they did to deserve their score. We think that's so we don't take it upon ourselves to decide their fate. Besides it is rarely obvious, you know unless you saw their murder trial on the news, dies next day and suddenly you're transporting them to level 7. What I can tell you is that the Colour of your skin, sexual preference, personal beliefs in Gods, foot fetishes. None of these are bearings on your level". I narrow my brow
"how can you tell that?" Dad smiles
"we have seen it all, Martin Luther King level one, Judy Garland level two, supposedly devout happily married white couple died in a car accident level 7. As it turned out KKK members thought they had rights above others had a very shady personal life. Man who murdered another man level 3, turned out he murdered the guy who raped and killed his daughter. The point is the once black and white rules for others, to a Pathfinder are

very, very grey so we can't judge. Not only that but we think it goes against us when it's our turn to be redeemed so it is best not take chances. That's what redemption is for, there is of course people over the years that have tried to write down their own versions of good and bad like Dante or what they think qualifies you for heaven. But they sometimes get a bit carried away with their own views, but that's information and stories for another day. James and I sit quietly for a minute trying to get our thoughts together,

"so why us?" James asks.

"Good question, to be honest no one really knows or remembers. We know it's fairly genetic, we know that over the next 5 years you're going to feel changes in your body you'll never expect and I'm not talking about things discussed in human biology classes. We are often stronger and faster than most people. We pick up certain skills and weapons naturally as though we have always known. Some theories have suggested we are all descendants of great and famous Pathfinders, Thor; Aphrodite; Anubis; Mars; Marilyn Munroe" I scoffed

"seriously?" dad looks over

"oh yeah she wasn't just beautiful, she had skills. Her death is less of a mystery to us as it is the rest of the world" James cuts in sounding sceptical

"I'm sorry Greek, Roman, Norse all these apparent gods were Pathfinders?" he was always clued up in history more than me.

"Yes" dad sits forward in his chair to explain "you see the magic and might of these people wasn't on earth, it was in hell. They were strong leaders and before there was a "standard uniform" they liked to wear their armour wherever they went, which is where a lot of civilisations get their ideas of how their deities looked. Some did take it too far and yes in many cases were worshiped, though it didn't always pan out well. Telling people that your special sparks a lot of jealousy and creates enemies. Nowadays we are not so quick to worship the first person with a few extra talents or tricks, but they were simpler times." I jump in excited "so we have magical powers?!" Grandad laughs "I wish"

19

Dad smirks too

"No. We don't know where a lot of the magic came from, some say it never happened and believe it may have just been their overly exaggerated skills. Others say we just forgot how, after all we still use some form of magic today or that it's just a slight miss interpretation of the weapons they used, we do have rune magic that we use a lot but you'll be taught how to use that later. As far as weapons are concerned today we use guns with silver bullets and explosives with silver shrapnel, but they run out of ammo fast so old school weapons are required. All recruits must be proficient in swords, shields, bows and all the other classics" "why silver?" James asks Dad who grins

"that is one of the few things Hollywood ever gets right, silver is kryptonite for most of the creatures of hell. Cuts them down like a hot poker through clover. Anyways that is enough for today, a week Monday I'm taking you two to your first training day, I think you will be surprised by some of your class mates".

Grandad pipes up and says to dad

"forgetting something lad?" Dad looks at him

"a yes of course" he pulls out two large boxes from behind the couch "this one is for you James and this one is for you Ryan" we opened the boxes to reveal two wooden swords that bore the same colour and markings as the box that contained our shields, Dad put his hand on my shoulder "that one was my sword Ryan when I trained" I looked at this battered and splintered sword with less awe than I think my dad was hoping for, James's sword looked in much better condition.

"And that one was my sword which is in better condition because I wasn't so reckless in my youth" Grandad looks at dad mockingly and pulls out two envelopes from his pocket. "Here you go boys spend it wisely" we opened the envelopes to reveal 100 pounds in each, five crisps 20 pound notes

"thanks Grandad" we both yelled. I wasn't wasting anymore time I ran up the stairs put the sword in my room, along with my small shield and headed down to the store to get my game.

# Chapter 3

## Coincidence

I'm not going to lie the rest of that day and a couple of days to follow, I was glued to my Xbox almost as though the events on my birthday didn't even happen. As luck would have it so were Simon and Brian. We met up online set up our fire team and lost track of time. James much the same pushed the events out of his mind and carried on messing with the old car in the garage, swearing when he's old enough to drive "this thing is gonna purr" he's always so sure of himself. Dad did however after a couple of days drag us outside for some sparing and fitness training before bringing out the swords and starting to show us proper techniques. During the week Simon and Brian had their birthdays too, but much the same as my own it came and went without much fuss or parties, which was strange all-round. Infact a few people in my year all had birthdays quite close by, which was common in the area. Most locals put this down to a 10 month delay following a certain local drinking festival, but curiosity did catch me by surprise. I got to school and caught up with the boys

"No party's lads? What did you two get up to for your birthdays this year?" I was half expecting two shrugged shoulders.

"not a lot mate hung out with the folks, couple random gifts you know lynx Africa and shit like that, not a lot really did grind a little online" Simon said with a subtle look away into the distance. Brian smiled at Simon "yeah my dad insisted we went for a family dinner, really messed up my game time" Brian grinned to himself. I know these boys enough to know when they are hiding something, but even more to know that usually plausible deniability is best, so I dropped the subject and carried on to maths class.

Most of the day was spent doing my usual, listening to the first five minute speeches about what we would cover today, only to realise I couldn't even remember what we did last time and blindly daze my way to the end of period. But the end of last the period before lunch gave me chills, seriously it was like the heating suddenly just dropped. I looked around to see if anyone else had noticed but no one flinched or shuddered like I did. I breathed heavily and noticed my breath was steaming in front of me, I was suddenly in a very cold room and the only one who could feel it. I was no longer sitting but standing up, the floor didn't feel solid and it was making a cracking sound like Ice splintering. I was looking all around me when I heard a voice as though in a distance, like a reptilian slither "we must close them all, we will have them and we will be free, it will free us all, find it, FIND IT NOW"

"Ryan, Ryan, RYAN!" I shook myself awake to see Mr Banks the history teacher along with the rest of the class staring at me.

"Sorry sir drifted off"

"well done Mr Campbell now if you could stay awake long enough to tell us when the armistice was signed you might avoid detention" Shit I can't even remember which war this is.

I spent that lunch break in detention trying to remember the dream, at least I think it was dream. Thinking about it in my mind the only thing I could really picture was the ice and what looked like spikes all around me. The voice was like an echo that didn't have an origin. What was it looking for? I tried to put it out of my mind. After all last week I had a dream I watched a fight between a Charizard and Toothless the dragon, now that's a dream worth contemplation.

Detention over, I went to my last class of the day and feeling sheepish I tried not to fall asleep. This was made easy as Brian and Simon kept teasing me about it for the rest of the day. Tomorrow is Wednesday and I get to attend my first day at the

Office. Keeping everything a secret from the boys is difficult, but thinking about what classes I will be attending there got me through the rest of the day. I wonder if I will be made captain when I graduate, what weapons I'll get to use and what my armour will look like.

# Chapter 4

## *Dumbstruck*

Mum was in the kitchen like always when I came down, the smell of fresh toast and butter filled the kitchen and the twins sat slurping their cereal. Today is the first day of official training and mum is getting all flustered

"Ok you have your lunch, your bag, your first aid kit, your phone, your shield and your Bokken" I looked glazed eyed at her through the sleep in my eyes

"what the hell is a Bokken" my dad walk in at this moment

"It's what you call a wooden practice sword sleepy head" He clipped my ear but I was too sleepy to reacted and just winced his way

"oryt, ok yeah it's here somewhere. At that moment the twins Lewis and Liam walk in followed by James. Liam looks up at dad "Daddy where are James and Ryan going? Why aren't they going to school with us? I want to go with them". Dad looks down at the two of them and chuckles

"They are going to school, just a different school. When you're old enough you will probably go to the same school too. Now finish your breakfast and let's get this show on the road, Campbell's are never late!" he raises his voice as though he was expecting some sort of hurried movement, we knew this was never going to happen.

We eventually made it into the car, James in the front with dad and me in the back staring into space. As we drive along I begin to consider the people in the world that have died

"Dad, have you ever taken anyone famous to their gate?" Dad

smiles as he reflects

"Yeah, actually remember my work trip to America last month, my team got to take Robin Williams to his gate. Sweet man only person I know that could make a decent through hell such a laugh. We had two other teams join the escort, It was more like an honour guard". I thought about this for a moment

"Your team?"

"Yes, pathfinders work in teams of six usually but can be more depending on the level required to descend to, its dangerous work no need go it alone if we can help it". We pull up outside the Red Lion which considering how many people work here seemed kind of empty. I asked dad

"where the hell does everyone park dad" he laughs

"you didn't think we all use the same entrance did you. The red lion pub is everywhere and many are used as an entrance to Purgatory from different parts of the country. It allows us to maintain our existence without drawing too much attention to ourselves. We just look like exceptionally regular and enthusiastic patrons to outsiders". Seeing the point of it I shrugged "what happens when a pub closes down?" I asked.

"It doesn't happen often as we own most of them and business is good, but sometimes a subtle word with the new owner helps. We do have other pubs as well and the occasional hair salon, but the bars are the most well-known. We walk inside the bar "morning Tony" said my dad. The bar man turns round to me and my brother

"best of luck today lads, I'll be seeing more of you two". We step through and dad turns to James

"go ahead son you can do it first". James steps forward and puts his hand on the door, standing tall as though he is about to give a speech

"Ne Obliviscaris", the bell ting followed by the white flash appears around the door then disappears. We stepped into the grand foyer and the awe came over me once again. We walked forward and joined the que at reception, James and I took a minute to take in the view again. It felt a bit like an airport terminal with people looking up destinations on over-head boards, only it was displaying random names, numbers and symbols with no destinations. The tannoy system made regular announcements, calling certain people to certain gates. The more we looked around the more we were trying to process. Different rooms lined the walls up and down levels with ebony signs and chrome plated words, Ethereal consultation, Bereavement affirmation, P.T.S.D Review centre, Pathfinder licensing bureau, Artefacts and so many others running up and down stairs. People with brief cases were shooting past in a hurry; groups of people in arrays of armour were grouping up and heading off into terminals at the far end of the room. "seriously we need a license to be a pathfinder?" dad looked over at the door "oh yeah, we had an incident a good few years ago couple of the office team decided to team up and take some souls through hell to find their gates, trying to prove they knew all about hell from their studies of the different trials and landscapes". I was worried to ask

"how did they get on?" Dad winces a little at the memory

"it wasn't pretty, out of 6 only two were retrieved and the souls they were escorting were lost. Of the survivors one retired and now spends his days writing government conspiracy blogs, bit of a tin foil hat kind of deal. The other works in accounting, she does a good job but the P.T.S.D. has her afraid of the photo copier, the doctor reckons it's something to do with the flashing lights and noises" I picture the machine operating and her cowering

"why weren't they fired or jailed" I asked

"HR for the most part got involved there, Office teams are rarely given the credit they deserve for the work they do, not that anyone says it but there is a deep rivalry between soldiers and clerics. It was felt they had already lost so much from the incident that new practises were put in place instead of punishments" James and I looked at each other. "Don't worry boys all will become clear and you have five years of training before the real fun begins" We got closer to the desk and the Receptionist spoke

"Next please" this was us. Dad collected his paper work and

walked us over to the training centre at the rear of the complex. The words "The Academy" were embossed in Silver onto a large ebony plaque over a large hall entrance. The academy was an annexed hallway that opened into a large circle around a central group of benches. Doors all around marked different classes from new recruits working up to Specialist classes

"right boys door on left is for new recruits, I have a job to do so I'll see you at reception when you're done good luck and mind your manners" he went to walk away then paused and looked back "if I'm a bit late don't piss off the receptionist they might not be Pathfinders but they are combat trained and beating the stupid out of someone isn't frowned upon" James and I looked at each other, smirked and said goodbye to our dad. Just as we went to open the door to go into class I heard

"DUDE!" I swivelled round quickly to see Brian and Simon the dynamic duo running towards me. I opened my mouth to answer but Simon spoke first "dude what are you doing here?" this needed mocked

"Got lost looking for the men's room in the pub came across this place, what you think I'm doing here? So your family too huh?" Simon looks at me with his Cheshire grin

"yeah turns out my family and Brian's family were Pathfinders in America, the reason we moved is our parents were head hunted for a transfer for this branch back in the day, they liked the area and stayed". Simon was from Nevada originally and Brian from Chicago their parents are Coveted Pathfinders. Brian's mum was sadly lost on a mission two years after moving but his dad decided to stay because his mum loved the area and people so much.

"Shall we?" James was growing impatient so we stepped into the class room. We entered the room and I looked around to see some familiar faces from school and some from induction day but most where strangers. There were around 60 people in the class in total all speaking different dialects and sticking in small groups. Now that I thought about it a good handful of the students that I recognised from my school were as good in P.E as James and I. Guessing their parents had them running drills from a young age too, a soft feminine voice sounded behind me "Move please your blocking the door" I turned round to apologise and was dumb struck. There she was, auburn hair flowing down her shoulders, blue eyes glittering by the soft fluorescent room light, lips like...I am thinking about this way too much, wait did she just say something? "gonnae move, yourin ma road". Beautiful, not delicate. I stepped aside and let her pass trying not to make smelling her perfume too obvious. Brian put his hand on my shoulder

"Well that's him broken for the next five years" I looked round at Brian who was sniggering as he said it

"shut up, where we sitting?"

A side door to the class room flew open "Morning class I am your Commanding Officer and trainer Lieutenant Williams you will address me as Sir or Lieutenant". A tall officer walked into the room rigid in her step with her emerald green eyes piercing every student in the class. Her uniform was flawlessly pressed with silver buttons polished to a fine shine running down the front of her uniform. Blonde hair tied up tight with not a strand out of place, a stout robust chest and legs that could crush diamonds supported her steel figure. We had no idea if we were to sit, stand or salute. One thing none of us mistook was that we were not about to back chat this woman, she looked like Ronda Rousey's angrier twin. Simon whispered

"This is the most confused and terrified erection I have ever sported" I tried desperately not to laugh at Simons comment, I tried so very hard. "Is something funny Cadet!?" I stuttered a little "No ma'am, Sir, sorry". She narrowed her eyes looking at me "Today you begin your training to become Pathfinders, Scholars or Clerics, not all of you will succeed. Those who are disobedient or not keeping up with the curriculum won't even make it into the Office cleaning staff. This is not a place for timewasters; we are dealing not only with the lives of you and your team mates but the future and fate of those passing out of this world. Families do not know what you do for their loved ones, nations do not know the demons we keep out of their plain and no one will be able to identify you if you screw about in my class!, is that clear!" Everyone in the class lightly muttered "Yes Sir"

"I SAID IS THAT CLEAR!!" We all joined in

"SIR YES SIR" We all believe she meant every word of it. "Take your seats, let the next five years begin".

"Who can tell me what it is that we do here?" James raised his hand and the LT nodded

"The safe guarding of Purgatory from demons of hell and the safe transportation of souls to their redemption gates" The lieutenant raised her eyebrows and nodded impressed

"Very good we are the guardians of this plain and the fate of those souls that wish to seek redemption from their sins". Simon was the first to ask

"what happens if they don't leave and stay in purgatory?" the LT looked over at Simon and narrowed her eyes

"Firstly cadet raise your hand to ask a question. From the moment a soul leaves the body it begins to fade. Most souls can last only about a week after death without reaching redemption, if they stay in Purgatory they fade from existence if they fade in hell they become creatures of hell, if captured they can be consumed or tortured for eternity. Before purgatory, souls had to cross the plain of hell by them-selves to find their gates, those that weren't consumed or taken by the demons would shrivel and turn to smaller hell creatures like imps, ghouls and hounds. Many of the more dangerous demons are still believed to have been human's before-hand but we are not sure on all of their origins. Now who can tell me the difference between the pure and those who require redemption?" To my delight Mia was the first to raise her hand

"Pure souls are mostly children but some rare adults do qualify, these are souls who have not committed any acts that require redemption. They are souls who do not require going into the depths of hell as their gate is on our level" The LT nods

"very good" The LT continues around the class "How do we

know what level to take those who require redemption too?" A girl I didn't recognise answered

"souls are marked with a Rune symbol on their arm, using this symbol we match the level and guide them to which level they are required to descend to in order to find their gate." The LT looks approvingly at the girl not anticipating Simon's interruption

"what if you already have tattoos? Can you see the mark?" LT Williams began to scarlet at this "Your last warning cadet" She continues "Souls don't have tattoos, piercings, scars, broken bones or handicaps in any way mentally or physically. Even those who died of old age feel young again, this is because you cannot harm or mark your soul, but you can corrupt it.

# Chapter 5

## The First look
### (2 Years on)

The next few years were intense, as well as attending regular school Monday and Tuesday, we had been in class and in training the rest of the week. Apparently due to the nature of our tuition the schools are given a government approved letters for each student, saying that we are attending a specialist programme and have authorisation to be away three days a week. As glad as I was I really wanted to know how much the government really knew of the operation. LT Williams didn't let up, every morning at 6am we had to report in for a two mile run followed by sparing and assault courses. The afternoons were all about different classes teaching us techniques and strategies to deal with any situation we came across. Resistance training was the toughest, it filtered a lot of personalities and skills separating Soldiers from office workers. Being able to deal with intense heats in full pack while scaling walls, staying awake for 48 hour periods while completing random tasks . Some weekends we were taken away up mountain ranges given a box of supplies mostly biscuits that made you constipated and orange juice that gave you the runs. It took weeks to figure out how to balance them and even longer before we found out how to sneak in energy bars. This box was all we were allowed until the end of the weekend along with a couple of bottles of water we had to share and ration. Sometimes we went to school looking forward to rubbish school dinners craving pizza and custard. The LT was tough but she wasn't the screaming "show me your war face" tough, most of the time she would help someone struggling and no-one wanted to let her down, there was never a single exercise she wasn't right by our sides spurring us on. She did finally manage to get Simon to raise his hand in class, it took several miles round the track and the fastest sparing sessions in history. Honestly no bruise ever hurt more than his pride. She was also able to make him an expert in hand to hand combat over time and his knife skills were becoming impressive. Naturally he loves to show off and can often be found on the range honing his throwing skills. Overall impressed by the speed our class's progression, more team members were allowed to take more specialists training ahead of their time. Even though some were destined for the Office, combat was still a must for everyone. Our Quartermaster Sargent Rogan, a portly man with a jolly demeanour was swooning over James for being so young but so skilled at the anvil. He had never seen anyone pick up tools with his finesse and was very quickly the class favourite for advice. This was easy jokes for Brian and Simon but they settled down when James showed them how to improve their armour and found listening bore brilliant results. Brian was doing really well too, his talents were more focused to the Marksman range. He was able to shoot 100 for 100 moving targets a record only achieved by one other Pathfinder at our Office, Captain Richard Campbell Aka Popps or grandad to James and I. It gave Brian and Grandad something to talk about when Brian came over for dinner and sparked a small rivalry that entertained everyone. My own talents didn't seem to manifest until we picked up swords. The sword of the Pathfinder is a double edged Carbon Steel blade, Edged with Silver mixed with soil from hell. This made it stronger than most alloys and unique to our order. I never felt more badass than the first time I picked up one of these swords and waved it around. We were only ever allowed to spar with our wooden swords and I was top of the class even when holding a shield it felt like an extension to my arm. The moments we got to test our skills with a real sword I let loose and felt every eye on me around the spring centre, I loved it. I kept going back in on the odd Saturday for private sessions in the combat arena, sometimes James would join me but Dad was my main sparring partner. I could see why everyone looked up to him, his stance though strong was fluid when he fought and his movements so precise he could cut a hair to the follicle and never break skin. This level of skill and commitment flowed out of him in his speeches and presence when commanding soldiers. Stuff I never noticed as his son and came to respect as I grew better.

Our little group over the few years had expanded, Chloe an expert in gate runes and symbols had taken a shine to Brian and we got the feeling it was mutual though he would never admit it and drop his guard. Chloe was from Ireland originally but moved over when she was a baby, dark hair over her shoulders when it wasn't tied up and with glasses over dark blue eyes. She stood around 5ft 6" making her the shortest in the group but by no means the quietest. Her knowledge of Runes and History was outdone by no-one not even James which made her a coveted study partner. Steven a local boy who spent most of his time in the local forests was an expert archer and field survivalist, who often preferred his own company he had dark short hair and despite the training he maintained a wiry frame which didn't detract from how deadly he was. There wasn't a person or creature he couldn't sneak up on without making a sound. It didn't take long before we took him into our group and he was always taking the lead on survival training. He also turned out to be expert tracker and scout for which he earned more than a few commendations. Others in the class took up studies such as soul studies, all about how to help souls come to terms with death and the next steps, administration studies and other Cleric specific roles. Demolitions were a popular choice amongst Pathfinders, but only a select few were ever permitted to move forward beyond basics. One person nearly took out the west wing of the complex, by playing with a lighter too close to his mix and spent two months of weekends cleaning classrooms. Everyone had to learn Demonic abilities and appearances, no-one wanted surprises so we didn't begrudge a little homework in the subject. History was very important but it was hard to remember and my scores weren't the best. The amount of mythology in the world is incredible and how similar they all are is even more so. The message they kept trying to reinforce with us was that you have probably heard of a person, demon or artefact you just know it or them by a different name. Although there were basic types of creatures we could all name, there was a focus on being able to identify ones from old folk lore, we required knowledge on old creatures from Werewolves, Vampires, Greek furies, Egyptian scarabs, Chinese Drakes and the Scottish pixies. Though no-one had seen these creatures in centuries it was believed that fore-warned is fore-armed.

We were reaching the end of a sparing class, one of the students was being tended too by the duty nurse when a man walks in and LT Williams asks us all to gather round.

"Stand at attention please. Now class this is Major Williams, yes to answer that look he is my big brother no further questions necessary" Major Williams was even taller than the LT with ash blonde hair and sporting the most impressive blonde moustache I had ever seen. He looks at the LT grins and looks back at us

"At ease, given the progress you have all made the LT has requested your class to move forward the date of your first expedition, to the Pure Gate" the class looked thrilled at this news, being able to finally enter hell and see what they were being trained for "This is to take place next Monday at 0800 hrs, anyone late can spend the next 30 years in the office counting newcomers at the arrivals gate. Enjoy your weekend, Dismissed" The scraping of chairs was quickly followed by the whispers of students all talking about rumours they had heard of hell. One thing we noticed across the board was that none of our parents had divulged what hell actually looks like or what happens.

The weekend flew by even new game content or the arrival of new alloy wheels for James's car which was really starting to take shape, couldn't stop the endless gossip about what was in store for us come Monday. No matter how much we pestered Dad or Grandad (no-one bothered mum she was the best at keeping secrets) they didn't let up, only to say it's not what you expect. I decided to take a walk down town to take my mind off things and hopefully settle my nerves, don't get me wrong I was excited, but actually entering hell did have me a little on edge.

I decided to take a walk into the town square, I passed some shops and stopped for a Mr whippy ice-cream, it has to be done. Nothing says nice day better than soft whip vanilla ice-cream and a Cadbury flake melting quicker than can be licked. I made my way towards the town statue. The Statue wasn't your typical statue, it was of the Old Duke riding a unicorn. The horse has the front two legs up suggesting he died in battle, this was amusing to most towns folk but I wanted to know (knowing what I know now) if this was a real moment in time. I was staring at the Duke when that horrible feeling came over me once again, that cold creeping over me like ice in my veins, I thought I was suffering the mother of all brain freeze. I looked around at the statue that was beside me, only it was rubble and the buildings around were crumbling and falling away. Colder and colder I was shivering all over, the ground around me once again began to crack and I was standing in a huge cavern. The feeling was starting to overcome me when I could hear a man's voice "I'm close my love I'm close I can feel it, it must be found it must" then that slimy forked serpent tongue began to speak

"good, find it, defile it and you will be rewarded" I shivered at the voice before a man spoke

"Yes I will, I will find it and we will be together again" The feeling faded and I blacked out. Next thing I knew I woke up still next to the statue to see a group of locals huddled around me, they were telling me I had fainted and they were going to call me an ambulance. Other than my pride I was unharmed if a bit shaken. I thanked them said I was fine and walked back home.

When I got back I spotted James in the garage, as always working away on the beetle, I shouted over

"Alright bro?" he looked up

"yeah I'm good where have you been dad wanted to get a spar in before dinner I reckon you can take him with your sword skills now" I gave a little smirk at this

"yeah ill show the old boy how it's done, here have you been hearing things recently? Or felt things get cold really quickly? Twice I've heard weird voices" James stops and looks at me a little puzzled

"not really, what do they sound like?" I thought about it

"honestly if I had to say it sounds like a back and forth between Golem and Voldemort's mother" as I said it even I doubted myself that it had happened

"too many movies mate, or not enough porn take your pick" I laughed

"dick head". I went inside and could smell it the moment I walked in the door, mums famous spaghetti bolognaise cooking on the hob and eve's pudding in the oven for dessert, culinary nirvana all thoughts of cold spots and deformed voices were forgotten.

The weekend didn't last much longer it felt like we were back in class and awaiting Major Williams's orders in no time. It wasn't long before the Lt and he strode into the head of the room in full weapons and armour. We got up from our desks and seats before the Lt spoke

"To attention!" we all stood upright "as you were" she then nodded to the Major

"now then, morning class before we set out a small reminder that although the top level is well guarded and the creatures are fairly basic more like rabid dogs than monsters, I must remind you that rabid dogs are dangerous too. Therefore we will be reporting to the armoury, you must be fully kitted even for your first run. Please report to the armoury, assemble your armour then report to the departures gate. Dismissed"

We wasted no time and Sargent Rogan was waiting our arrival in the armoury

"you know where to go, can finally see if you've been paying attention to detail, James I want you front and centre when you're kitted out". Our lockers were all kept in the armoury for security reasons along with the changing rooms, girls and boys separated of course. The armour of Pathfinders is mostly a black anti-stab material slightly stronger than Kevlar and used instead of metal plating except for the chest plate, shin plates and gauntlets. This was to allow more movement, it didn't breath much but against blades and sharp teeth it worked a charm. Most chose to wear a black cloak that could be draped over the head, this was useful as one way round. It had amazing silver designs and runes, but flipped round you could shroud yourself in a pitch black and never be seen. Throughout the armour there is real silver thread woven into patterns and runes are used to protect from heat, spells and other demonic forces. Most symbols were mandatory to have included in designs but Chloe showed us few extras that we each felt would come in handy. James and I had both emblazoned a hogs head on our chest piece, except we went for a modern geometric design instead of the family crest. When our hoods were up we looked awesome like two rangers of middle earth. The Majors, Colonels and all ranking officers were given Solid Silver gauntlets and accompaniments that were engraved with their Chevrons or stations emblem, although their stations were supposed to be a supervisory role no one believed they were less equipped for battle. James soon got ready and the designs he had chosen were arguably very impressive with flawless details, his sword was the finest the Quartermaster had seen and stronger than he could make himself. James was more ready for a fight than any of the rest of us, even though this wasn't his final work far from it. One team member who's skills definitely did not lie on the field or in the armoury went to put his arm through his sleeve only to rip the arm right off. After a few laughs from the class and the Sergeant inspecting the rest of his work with little compliment, he was sent to get the spare out of the back lockers. Once dressed for the part we made our way through to the foyer to the Departures gate. As the souls passed by us the silver in our armour glowed slightly. This made the walk to the gate that little bit extra cool.

The Major took us too our door and stopped, the LT was behind us keeping everyone close "very simple, enter one by one do not hover, just pass through and join your class mates" the door was a giant steel disc that rolled back from the opening revealing the portal, we couldn't shut down the gates but this was a good alternative. The entrance was a stone arch that was edged with several runes and symbols that glowed brightly. Once open it revealed a veiled mist sunken from the doorway. Simon sniggers "I knew it Sirius Black isn't dead he's been here the whole time" Major Williams was another who didn't miss anything "Mr Peters if you wouldn't mind going first" I knew Simon shit himself at this, also how did I go this long not knowing his surname was Peters. Simon stepped forward, he stared into the mist took a deep breath, entered and then disappeared. We stared for a second watching the Major follow Simon through before being ushered forward, one by one each class member entered until it came to my turn. I took my step forward and felt the cold rush of the mist pass over me then suddenly, I was in the town square, at least for a split second it looked like I was. The walls and battlements were all the same except from the extra roads and passages that had been added. Where there were shops in our realm was ammo storage, weapon emplacements and troops gathering equipment. The towers and battlements had soldiers patrolling on them in regular circuits. I looked up at the sky, there was a sun but it was misted as though a permanent fog lay in front of it, no blue sky just constant cloud. The air was close but a soft breeze made its way through the courtyard and the smell of ash wisped my nostrils. Looking over towards the centre the town statue was missing, there was just a path from the wall arch and portal behind me cutting straight through the square to the exit on the far side out of town. Troops marched in formation and sentry's patrolled all around. We waited until the last person stepped through before Major Williams spoke "Welcome to hell, with any luck this is a pleasant surprise, Hollywood does like to make it look a bit bleaker than it really is. This is the Pure level or level 0 to some, it is a mirror image of our world, to a certain extent, there are of course some differences. Brathaidh is the main base of operation for the British branch of purgatory due to its strategic infrastructure so those of you who are local to the area may recognise a few things. Now then, Cadet Henderson isn't it, I know your mother well, fine soldier, can you tell me the time please?" Lisa takes out her phone to check but it was completely dead, to be honest I don't know why I expected low bars, the major spoke triumphantly "that's right dead, electrical devices of any sort do not work in this plain which makes the building of fortifications and operation of the Seal a completely manual job. Heavy utilisation of the runes and symbols combined with rudimentary incantations is how we communicate and interact with our surroundings that is why it's important some of you excel in the role of Scribes. Remember the ancients called it magic, with every step forward we call it science." I looked up thinking about what he said

"Sorry Sir the seal?" Major Williams looked at me "someone's paying attention, suppose I should expect as much from you young Master Campbell. This way cadets!" The Major lead the way out of the Fortress entrance, through the great gate and past the old Cathedral outside of town. We walked until we reached an open field on the edge of town. One of the cadets from my town spoke up

"Sorry sir where is the lake?" The Major spun round to address the cadet

"On our plain this is a lake but here it is the location of our great seal, lakes or lochs as they are in Scotland are great places to hide such important structures as in hell there is often very little water inland

"is there water elsewhere?" blurted another cadet, the Majors eye twitched

"Yes believe it or not hell does still have some basic resources though nothing grows here. There are seas, lakes and rivers however I wouldn't recommend swimming in them and they are not very safe and you should never consume them. As for structures we have to imbue all metal structures with soil from this land so that they don't corrode at the rate of most things here, standard stainless steel untreated will last around two weeks before becoming an orange pile of rust. Even steel that is treated turns in around a year or so. Constant maintenance is required at sights, the only metal safe is Silver alloyed with the soil which as you know is what your equipment is made from" The Major gestures us onwards and soon we approach the Seal surrounded by Pathfinders on guard duty. In the middle was a 30ft wide metal circular plate with 4 large chains linked at 4 symmetrical points. On the plate is 10 very large engraved runes and symbols that were glowing a bright white and an outer ring glowing around the edge, only a few of the symbols I recognised from our studies. "Now then, who can tell me what these represent?" the Major looks round at the class, we all knew Chloe would be the one who knew and the Major gave her the nod to answer as she waved her hand

"Sir, the 9 around the edge represent the different levels of hell but the 10th in the middle remains a mystery as no record of it can be found or matched, there are theory's but given that the symbol is a sword and many have existed over the centuries it is all speculation and the main theory is that this is the symbol for the Pathfinders themselves" the major looks on impressed

"correct the tenth has had many theories over time being called the last gate or the last barrier, but no one has ever figured out its true purpose at least not in the last few centuries. Ah very good right on schedule" The Major gestured to the route we just travelled to get to the seal. 6 Pathfinders followed by 5 souls made their way towards the seal. The Captain of the group passed his documentation to the lead guard for authorisation, at this the Major told us all to move back. The Pathfinder and souls stepped onto the plate, at that moment the leader of the guard ordered the sentry's around the seal to aim their weapons so that they covered every inch of the edge of the seal. With a large clunk, the plate begun to lower slowly. I couldn't really tell from our vantage point but I guessed they must have been lowered a good 40ft before the chains stopped moving. After 5 minutes the chains began to move again and the seal was returned to its resting spot sealing the chamber "well there you have it class another team off to do their duty" at this the whole class became a flurry of questions, not least of all the questions I had of my own " yes, yes I know you all have questions but this is not the time nor the place. Now that you have all seen the seal we are going to make a quick trip to the Pure Gate" no one pushed their questions as the Pure Gate was something everyone wanted to see. We travelled back to the edge of town and came to the towns Cathedral which sat 300 yards off the southern wall. More guards were posted around it making constant tours around the building. Before I knew it, words escaped my mouth "Sir, I thought we didn't bother with churches and the like" I thought the major was going to go scarlet with the amount of questions but he was obviously waiting this question "yes its true we do not wrestle with the religions of the modern or historic world but we have found that putting these gates in buildings that are protected and not likely to be taken down provide a strong anchor to our plain that we can imbued with our protection both in hell and earth, it's a good method of preservation and fortification. We don't just use churches, we use other religious buildings and parliament buildings. Anywhere we think a suitable mirror of our plain will manifest works well to set up our gates. Unfortunately when the building is destroyed on earth it eventually fades here which is why we put certain protections on them" James grasped my impatience "Sorry Sir are you saying we make the Gates?" the major obviously less patient now and deepening his tone

"The purity gate can be set up anywhere we choose owing to the nature of those that enter them, we set them up along what is known as the Rose lines or Lay Lines. The Rose lines are spiritual lines that intersect at certain points on the world map. Using runes in specific combinations we can set up the gates on the level where we desire. The gates below however because of the way the landscape changes and nature of the souls, we cannot set up gates where we choose and therefore those already created before our charge must be simply located. We use runes to set up pure gates above, locate the gates needed below and to communicate with each other. Thankfully we have been able to modernise how the runes function and how we can use them to our advantage, instead of carrying around pebbles and stones in cloth bags, the Scribe carries around what looks like a Cryptex. In place of a gauntlet on their left arm, the device is secured much like a cylinder with padding. We call this the Enigma Gauntlet though other sites have their own names. The runes are small fastened in 10 loops the first 5 containing the alphabet the second magical symbols, supporting 26 runes per loop and secured so they can be spun into different combinations, the wearer is then able to spin the runes into the combinations they require. Depending on what combination you require and the correct words or incantation, you can send messages to other Pathfinders, look at the gate activations locations and other uses. It was even said that the elders knew combinations to open special routes inside the labyrinth below". We were approaching the Cathedral when I begin to feel the aura coming from within the building, it feels like cool air brushing over my skin in pulses. As a class we enter the cathedral and walk into the main hall. Where there would usually be rows of pews was an empty room and all around was stone pillars and stone work intricately carved. A huge stained glass window was at the back illuminating the room in different coloured lights, where there would usually be an altar, was the stone arch with the pulsing misty portal we knew to be the Pure gate. We began to gather in front of the arch, it stood roughly 8ft tall 5ft wide made of what looked like the darkest obsidian rocks and silver runes are engraved all round "now you see where we get our colour scheme" the Major smiled, the class looked on in awe as the white light pulsed from the gate. It was a few minutes before Joseph one of our class mates spoke

"Sir why is it none of the bigger demons and creatures just attack us and destroy the gate?" the Major was about to answer when a scribe or Rune Master as they were sometimes referred appeared from behind the gate. Master Marcus the leader of our branch's scribes wore not a cloak as we did but a set of black and silver robes. They didn't trail on the ground like an old wizard robes, these were well fit robes that locked using a belt in the front and with a silver scroll on the left chest symbolising their scribe order "that is because of the purity of those souls we protect, this gate and all those across the world combined with the seal and the seals used by the others create an aura all round that constantly pulses. The smaller demons are not as threatened by the pulse of the pure gates but the closer the greater demons of hell get to the surface, the weaker they become before they are destroyed altogether" Simon chuckles

"sooo pure souls are demon kryptonite" the Master smiles

"so they are, we use silver to channel this energy, it gives us our strength and gives our weapons the kick they need to smite our foes. And of course the black, never goes out of style" Master Marcus chuckles at his joke.

We got to have a look around the Cathedral and speak to the rune master before a team came in with some souls. Two boys and little girl all holding hands walked in between the soldiers, the reality of what we were doing and why we were doing it began to press on all our minds. If we didn't do our jobs, they would have lived a short life and followed up with an unpleasant afterlife. by simply fading from existence or being torn apart by some demon. We protect them so that they have a chance, to have another chance. The Major spoke up "back up everyone please don't want anyone stepping into the gate that isn't suppose too, that is a one way trip" We watched as the leader of the group spoke to the kids, they didn't looked scared it was like they knew what was going to happen. The leader stood up and sent them through holding hands, an all-mighty pulse of white light shot out of the gate and the silver on everyone's armour and weapons glowed a phosphorescent white light that surged through our body's before slowly dimming away.

They are safe now,

But there are more every day that need us,

We have a job to do.

We headed back to the Office once we had been to the armoury and removed our gear, we went into the class room to gather our things. The Major wanted us to take the rest of the day off, he said it was to come to terms with the task ahead of us. He wasn't wrong, no one had spoken much on the way back from the gate, somehow seeing the kids, knowing they didn't have much of a life but were being given a chance in death got everyone thinking.

Mia came up to James and I who were just about to head to reception and wait on dad "don't know about you two but I'm motivated more now than ever, Its time we grew up and did what we were born to do". Just like that she left the room leaving James and I looking at each other.

She was right, it was time to grow up.

# Chapter 6

## *Level one and two*
### (1 Year on)

No one let up, we pushed harder and harder until the distinction between those destined for the office and those for the field became unarguably obvious. For those of us who chose to become Pathfinders, once we had passed basic and advanced combat training we were given private status and able to go on combat experience to levels one and two. Brian, Chloe and I were first to go to level one and got to join a crew heading down with 3 souls. Our superiors hadn't found out or had chosen not to acknowledge the relationship between Brian and Chloe so they were allowed to go together, they didn't show any sign of it in the office so I didn't expect anything awkward in the field. We went to our lockers where our gear was waiting, it took me 20 minutes to get it right, I didn't want a stitch out of place for my first run. I removed inspected then sheathed my sword on my left side, listening to that satisfying shift of metal. On my right hip was my side arm and an assault rifle on my back, taking a moment to look at myself in the mirror with my hood up, a grin grows across my face. The years had been kind my physique was more pronounced, my stature more rigid and smooth skin adorned what could one day be a fine beard. Staring at the mirror into my own eyes I say "today I make a difference". Brian came round the corner from his locker with his sniper rifle strapped to his back, his sword was smaller than standard allowing speed over power in case he was ambushed while sniping he told me this was called a Gladius after the swords wielded by romans. He also had a side arm on the hip but in practise he rarely used it, with his sniper skills nothing ever came close enough in train-ing to warrant its use. We headed out into the hall where we met up with Chloe who was waiting and talking to one of the troops taking us down. Chloe had the robes of the scribe instead of the Pathfinder cloak. This didn't mean she had chosen an office life, scribes were used just as much in the field as we were because they held the Enigma Gauntlets. This device was key to keep-ing in contact with the Surface, Office and finding Gates below level. I looked her up and down

"not bad, the robes suit well" she grinned said thank you then looked at Brian for approval who didn't seem to be able to form words, this didn't matter Chloe knew he wasn't articulate when it came to pretty girls so took the silence as the compliment. Captain Fraser one of the Offices best Pathfinders approached us "are you all ready to go privates?" we each nodded and followed behind her through the portal. The walk to the seal didn't seem to take long at all and I fought to keep my nerves under control as we approached. I stepped onto the seal and with no word of a lie I was terrified, but I kept my cool quite well as we were lowered down. With each clang of the metal chain I was just thankful I wasn't claustrophobic, the closeness of the air began to push on me the further down we went and the smell of hot ash became more prevalent in the pit. We were lowered until we started to reach the bottom, the seal slowed down before coming to a sudden stop on the chamber floor. Once we had all stepped off the seal I noticed that the silver of our armour was glowing and lighting the room, I knew this was because we were close to souls but I never realised this was actually the light we used when in the tunnels. We were given specialised oil lamps for when necessary as battery torches were useless in hell. I don't know why, but how dark it was going to be never crossed my mind and I was thankful to have the light created by the souls. The noises coming from all round were a little un-nerv-ing, it was really quiet and yet it felt like nothing was standing still. The Captain of the troop started talking to the souls I'm guessing to make sure they were feeling ok, while she did that the Duty Scribe was spinning the symbols on his gauntlet until he found the ones he was looking for,+ making sure Chloe saw what he was doing "remember once you have chosen them lock them down and make sure only the runes you need are touching, don't want any random incantations" once he spoke the spell to activate the gauntlet, the lock on the gauntlet lifted and the runes began spinning. He began slowly turning round before locking on one tunnel "it's this way for these two". It took a couple of hours in the tunnels a couple of imps tried to come at us but the troop took them down in seconds. We spotted the gate we needed in the distance before a couple of demons emerged, they looked like burnt men with swords straight out of the kiln, one had large chunks missing out of its shoulder but that didn't seem to impede it. They started running at us, just as the Captain was about to make a move Brian dropped both of them

"where the hell did that come from?" asked one of the soldiers turning round, Brian shrugged "see evil, shoot evil, walk away like a badass". He's not wrong, that was fucking awesome I just didn't see him even raise his rifle it was that fast though my ears were now ringing with the echo "noise discipline please, it was a good shot Private but now the whole neighbourhood knows where we are" Brian's smile drops and he bows his head

"yes sir, sorry sir". We got to the gate, un-like the kids these souls were told to go in one by one. The first soul went in and the same as the kids the light flashed but not quite as bright as the kid's gate, apparently the less pure the soul less bright the light is. The second soul went in and we waited, but there wasn't the flash in-fact it was more like a brass clang.

"What was that?" I said, the leader looked at me

"we don't really know, but the theory is that, that was someone not passing redemption. We guess not everyone can be redeemed or wants to be redeemed for their actions, or they chose a different route. No idea, either way they made it and our job is done" The scribe started moving his Gauntlet again

"this way, also message from the office one crew has returned saying they had hell hounds on their route and were unable to remove them all" The walls were well grooved into the landscape. Sometimes with shaped soil, sometimes stone carved through, some passages stood near 10ft in diameter others had us walking in single file to get through. It only took 45 minutes to reach our last gate and the last soul was through before long. Using our oil lamps we had just about made it back to the seal when I heard growling, 8 of them appeared from different directions,

"keep it tight weapons up or drawn, work in your pairs they will go for the throat if they can don't let the rest of your guard down either. It was a standoff that felt like it lasted ages until the first dog ran forward, we cut or shot most of them down before one of them sank its teeth into the ankle of one of the troops, I span round after cutting my one down and buried my sword in its skull and watched it drop to the floor then fizzle to ash which the demon soldiers and imps didn't do

"Since when do dogs do that?" I said and the Captain came up to me

"Some do, we don't know what it means some think it was a good soul that was trapped and has been released to the next life other think they are the worst of them" She looks at the injured cadet being treated now by Chloe

"of course all dogs do go to heaven right" I laughed to myself at this reference. We managed to carry the Finder to the seal and the scribe called the plate down. It was a good first adventure and the Finder only required some minor stitches and R&R. Thankfully and largely down to the fabric of his armour. It still took a while for me to stop shaking but the Captain assured me it was just the adrenaline of the fight, before thanking me for saving her team member.

Other teams went after us and within a couple of months we were being sent to level 2 as well. Most of us went without any major problems, James had a Fury on one of his runs, a large winged creature in a chamber tried to swoop down and take a soul. He quickly spun round parried the creature away with his sword before putting his pistol to its eye socket, squeezing the trigger and watching it drop. This got him a commendation as not only were Fury's usually hard to deal with but he didn't flinch in his duty the whole time. Most others encountered ghouls, imps and undead soldiers. We did have the occasional person in the infirmary but no fatalities thankfully. Learning how to interact with the souls so that our runs were easier was important, we learned that they have no sensitivity to temperature and no desire or need for food and water. They could hold objects but it was recommended they didn't some souls especially lower level souls were as weak and susceptible to silver as demons were. I did have one corrupt soul try to make a break for it but being held at sword point got him to his gate.

After a year of level one and two we were all very confident with our weapons and 6 in our class were re-assigned to Field Scribe, naturally Chloe was head of the class in that field. We were finally in our Graduation year and LT Williams aimed to make sure we were the best she had trained yet. The exams were both physical and mental, naturally I excelled more in the former than the latter but my scores were fair. James, Mia and a few of the others proved to have more of an all-round skill set and proved to have particular proficiency in leadership skills. They were able to solve problems or utilise their teams well to solve puzzles giving them glowing scores.

# Chapter 7

## Graduation
### (2 Years on)

It was a tough 5 years all together, each of us growing into the strong confident adults we now were and holding our responsibilities in highest regard. Well mostly, when we had the occasional weekend off some days were a bit of a black out as work hard party hard was the groups mentality. Lt Williams I'm pretty sure she knew every time we felt a bit, tender. Her favourite "duty" was sending us to work in the rifle range, there are no headphones in the world that can shield you from the punishing sound those rounds being fired against the targets make, it was like having a frozen Toblerone rammed between your ears repeatedly.

The group hadn't changed much over the years and honestly I thought it would. Alcohol, intense training and different courses can have its toll on friendships and relationships but we remained close. Simon and Brian were actually renting a flat together in town which I regularly frequented, James and I still lived at home but rarely made an appearance, we were often either, work, pub or the boys place. James had become a lot more sociable and was seen out a lot with everyone. That was until one time I was given a weekend patrol duty in the office and a number of cadets had gone for a night out in town. It was 1 month later when my brother finally admitted to me he and Mia hooked up and they were now dating. Talk about a punch to the nuts, don't get me wrong I had never made a move over the years and she never paid much attention to me outside of the sparing arena, so I shouldn't have felt so surprised she was with someone else, but my own brother? A part of me wanted to be ok with it especially when I hooked up with another cadet two weeks after I found out about them, but things between James and I were tense and conflicted for some time after. He achieved a commendation for his work in the armoury and was going to lengths to upgrade my armour as a peace offering, it was working until he was made team leader of our group then I couldn't look at him without feeling very envious.

I did decide to date a local girl for a while but it didn't pan out well, one night I got invited to her house for dinner with her parents. I was going quite well, Mum was lovely and her Dad didn't try to square up to me, then again the bearing you get after years of combat training does tend slow most people down. We were sitting down to dinner when her mum took out the oven, the most burnt pie I have seen in my life, charcoal with filling doesn't cut it. The pie was served with the usual trimmings carrots peas etc, I started to poke the slice of pie on my plate when her dad said

"don't you normally say a prayer before eating young man?" I was lost in my curiosity at this burnt offering

"no my mum knows how to cook" It got very tense very quick and I couldn't choke down my dinner quick enough, we're still friends but her parents don't like me and apparently I'm not invited to dinner again. Simon and Brian are as ever thick as thieves and are quite passionate about their skill sets, Simon was maintaining his bachelor lifestyle and has never missed an opportunity to show off his knife skills or exceptional collection of dad jokes. Outside of the office he took up parkour and could be found jumping all round town along the battlements and Cathedral much to the local authorities dismay. Brian had become quite serious with Chloe, there was even a pregnancy scare at one point, but apparently an aggressive desire to eat ice-cream isn't a sure fire way to determine if someone is pregnant. On the range Brian was commended as the fasted and most deadly marksman the Lt had ever seen, this praise was lost on Brian though, he would rather spend 2 hours calibrating his scope than 2 minutes being told how good he was. Chloe was definitely the smartest in the class there wasn't a rune combination she couldn't recite and after never failing to impress the Rune Masters, she was given a scribe commendation and was given access to restricted archives for further research. She was a big asset to our study groups and really got Brian out of his shell on nights out. Steven who had come out of his shell a lot more as well was often seen with the group having a laugh, but he still liked to spend most of his down time hiking if he could get out of town for a bit. Having spent some time hiking around the Scottish highlands myself we bonded quite well about camping stories. Others to our group were Jason our accomplished demolitions expert who often loved to tell people if you see him running best keep up, Dixon who was great with assault rifles and helped everyone with calibrating theirs. Sarah who was an expert in sword and shield combat (almost as good as me) and Arwa another scribe student often joined our excursions.

By the time we finished our training Simon was promoted into a Lance Corporal, Brian and I were made Corporals and James was promoted to Sargent. Mia was also promoted to Sargent; she didn't fail to impress our commanding officers and her abilities with a fighting spear were second to none.

After initial training in the first 4 years we were organised into units, each troop was appointed an experienced Captain to lead for the first year on expeditions to levels 3 & 4. Yes even after we passed the first 4 years and levels there was still another year of training in levels 1-4 we had to do before we got to join the big leagues at 5+. It made sense I suppose, Our Captain was a Cpt Marshall who lead with his own Scribe, James, Myself, Simon and Sarah. Brian was in another troop with Mia, Chloe and a few others Jason, Arwa and Dixon were in another.

Despite what would still technically be continued training afterwards, the first 5 years were over and we were going to be going to our graduation ceremony. This meant that the armour and weapons we had been working on for 5 years were finally our own and we took a lot of pride in our handiwork. Although each Finder wore the same black material and silver embroidery, how we utilised the silver and worked the metal was individual to each Finder, supposedly when we make our own it's stronger than any passed on. My chest piece which had the Geometric Boar on the shield was well received by the C.Os and other team members who decided to look into their family histories for symbols.

In addition to our armour we are required to fashion and maintain our own weaponry, naturally I have my sword and took a long, long time trying to get it right. Pride doesn't even cut it, the Boar I engraved into the metal was flawless and balance of the hilt to tang was impeccable, yes I love it, it is perfect ... but if I'm honest, James's sword looks really bad ass too and I can't help but feel a little envious of his handy work which I knew was stronger than my own. Although a miniature engraving of a VW beetle next to the hilt was a bit much. We each have to carry at all times a Scar assault rifle and a Rhino 357 side arm and a sword standard or shorter. Brian favorited the M308 sniper and he spent much of his downtime calibrating his scopes. At least anytime he wasn't cuddled up with Chloe, as if we didn't know. Mia preferred a specialised fighting spear, Simon his knives as many as he could carry different shapes and sizes. Steven was our competent archer and most of the others chose to carry the standard sword often with shield. The Shield was a smallish round Targe style design, easy to carry and mostly silver alloy but painted black in spots to keep in with our look.

Graduation day approached fast, Grandad made the trip over and mum insisted on buying a new hat for the occasion, this was a running joke in the family as mum loved hats for special occasions but never remembered to take them to the events, so many never left their boxes. Dad, James and I went along to the office early so we could all get our armours polished and assembled in plenty of time. Apparently we couldn't get anyone to look after the boys so Dad had to get a special request authorised for the day, for Lewis and Liam to come to the Office. Who were being threatened upon death to misbehave at the ceremony, even though they had no real idea what was going on or where they were. There was a massive turn out in a year of 130 cadets from different classes. 70 became Pathfinders, only 10 Scribes and the rest joined office personnel. I looked around the lobby and saw mum persuading the twins into the auditorium dad ran over to give her a hand, James and I started to walk over to the side entrance and joined the que of class mates where we would be called forward and presented with our graduation certificate and ranks. We stood quietly for the most part then James spoke first

"so this is graduation huh, at least we don't have those stupid square hats. I think our outfits are a bit classier too" I gave a smirk at this, his gear was always looking tidier than my gear but I tried not to let it show. I looked over to the gates and saw some troops heading out with some of the latest souls, a sudden rush of pride and excitement came over me at the thought of one day commanding my own team.

The que whittled down slowly until I was to be called next, just as I was stepping forward I spotted someone slipping in behind the crew heading through the gates. The figure had the full armour but looked slightly hunched, still quite nimble though. I was about to comment before I heard

"RYAN CAMPBELL" from the podium, I marched forward towards the Commander smiling at me. "Achieving the roll of Corporal, Ryan Campbell" Two silver chevrons were handed to me to be sewn onto my shoulder and I was given a round of applause before stepping down to join the others.

"JAMES CAMPBELL" called the Commander, James stepped out and I could see my mums face beaming, "attaining the role of Sargent, James Campbell" only 5 people were promoted to Sergeant no-one ever got promoted to Captain out of training but James came close. As the Commander handed him his 3 chevrons I suddenly felt a red cloud over me, I wanted to lash out at him, the applause got louder and louder making the mist darker until I heard Brian's voice "dude move over" I snapped to my senses just in time to stop myself shouting out loud. What the hell was that? At that moment someone started shouting

" I can't stand it, none of you deserve this your all disgusting parasites" It was Cynthia from accounting who got up and stormed out with all eyes on her. James walked down from the podium and leaned towards me

"that's the one dad said went into hell a few years back and didn't turn out right" The Commander composed herself and was about to call the next person when more noises distracted the ceremony.

Some screams of fear started coming from the lobby and they got louder and until the main tannoy and alarm system started "ALERT, GATE BREACHED, ALL PATHFINDERS RESPOND" the tannoy repeated as we ran out to the lobby to find a swarm of imps were crawling all over the place trying to bite people and attack staff. I drew my sword and cut down seven in quick succession as fast as I could, I could hear Major Williams shouting

"all civilians and unarmed personnel head to arrivals Cap't Jennings Cap't Ashford get your squads and guard them" I could hear shouting everywhere as I moved to catch some more imps trying to crawl into the reception podium. Then I heard my mum's voice above everyone "LEWIS! WHERE IS LEWIS! LEWIS!" My dad ran over

"I will find him you get to arrivals with the others

"So I fucking will" she grabbed my dad's spare sword from its sheath and cut down three imps in one swing, I looked at Simon "Simon can you take Liam, take him to arrivals and look after him while we try to find Lewis" he nodded and we began to search everywhere for Lewis. It didn't take long before the imps were cut down, only a few minor injuries and the odd lost finger but otherwise unscathed.

We began moving around the offices checking for stragglers and Lewis, I was just marking off an office door as checked when I heard my mother scream. I sprinted to a small office for Enigma Gauntlet repairs, I stopped in the door way and all of a sudden

55

I couldn't feel my legs. On the ground was an imp with its neck snapped thrown against the wall, next to it were two legs. Two little legs, with tiny trainers, grey trousers and odd socks. Just lying there still and lifeless. I could hear my mum sobbing knelt down on the ground next to him

"not my baby, not my little baby, please not my little baby" I tried to move forward just as my dad ran in to see what had happened. He walked in and buckled down on his knees beside Lewis, dad moved closer and then picked up Lewis and held him in his arms

"No, no, no I should have been there, I should have been, my boy I'm sorry, I'm so sorry" tears ran down his face and landed on Lewis's chest, dad cuddled him close as though looking for a heartbeat and just rocked him slowly, Mum pressed her head to his whispering through tears. Lewis's eyes were closed as he lay motionless huddled in my dad's arms not in pain or scared just motionless as though asleep. I stood paralyzed, my little brother... was gone.

# Chapter 8

## *Shutdown*

It felt like hours I just stood there, I could feel the tears welling up and running down my cheek. No movement or speech came to me, my mouth was dry and my limbs numb. I tried to move but my muscles and limbs were alien to me. James was now in the room holding his head to Lewis's, tears were on his face too and he didn't make any sound. I kept searching my mind for words, then one came to me and I shouted it out loud without realising "ARRIVALS" I rushed out of the room and sprinted to the arrivals gate. I began shouting out "Lewis! Lewis! Lewis!" passing people who struggled to get out of my way quick enough, my head swivelled quickly to and fro looking franticly for him and then all of a sudden, there he was just standing there, looking around him bemused. He looked lost and scared as other souls passed by him, as I walked forward he spotted me and stared absently. I picked him up and took him in my arms holding back tears and holding him close then took him to one side. The first thing that came to mind was to say are you ok? but I knew in my head this wasn't the words he needed to hear, this came out instead "you muppet" he looked at me and his face gleamed

"no you're a muppet" I chocked a laugh then hugged him close again. James run over and he instantly hugged Lewis tightly as well resting his head on Lewis's shoulder

"what were you thinking running off are you ok?" Lewis smiled

"I'm ok but that monster was mean he bit me and scratched me"

James looked up at me then at Lewis

"Lewis you know you're" I could see James wrestling with what to say in his mind "a soul now don't you?" James said it as though hoping that maybe somehow Lewis knew what was going on, Lewis looked up at us

"what's a soul? And where's mummy and Liam?" James and I stared at each other, I didn't know what to say or how to explain this to him. All I knew is that I wasn't leaving his side until he was through the purity gate and safe. Mum and dad ran over, mum carrying Liam and more tears were coming down their faces as they spotted Lewis. The sobbing didn't stop as dad tried to consul mum and delicately explain to Lewis what happened what had happened. The Commander appeared with her guards "Major and Mrs Campbell I've just been told what happened I can't imagine how your feeling I..." Dad cut her off before she could finish

"how did they get through the gate? Where were the defences? Why and how were we attacked?" the Commander looked startled, dad didn't do it often but when he was mad he could intimidate anyone with a look and hold anyone to attention

"please come to my office this isn't a conversation for out here" Dad nodded, Mum stayed back with Lewis and Liam, not wanting to leave their sides for a second. I asked Brian and Simon to guard them, they both stood to attention weapons drawn guarding as though another attack could happen at any moment.

Dad, James and I went into the Commander's office and sat down she looked at James and I "Now what I'm telling you isn't strictly for you two but given the circumstances" an officer knocked on the door then walked into to the room

"sorry Commander you asked for me" the Commander nodded and gestured a seat next to us

"this is sergeant Macdonald he was at the cathedral when this kicked off and we are still getting reports as to what happened elsewhere. There aren't many witnesses to what happened outside the portal as we were on low guard for the ceremony, that reminds me before I forget" she turned to one of her guards "please check with Major Williams make sure all scout, patrol and active and off duty teams are recalled, I want fortifications doubled inside and out" The guard nodded

"yes sir" and left the room. The Commander took a deep breath then turned to the Sargent "Sargent please tell us what happened".

"I was walking around the cathedral doing my normal route when I spotted a squad was énroute to the Seal, behind them was a Finder but he was slightly behind as though keeping his distance, he was kind of hunched and limping. He had the uniform so I didn't give it much thought, he then must have changed direction from the squad as when came back around the building I saw the squad again in the distance but he wasn't there, he must have headed into to the cathedral when I wasn't looking. I was heading around the corner to sweep the rear side of the building again and just as I was coming back around there was a great horn sound that shook everything, then a huge blast of light and all the windows of the cathedral shattered blasting out. I was knocked off my feet but got back up quickly when I could hear shouting as the imps swarmed the Fort, I've never seen so many they were like ants over a leaf. It was as though the blast was their signal to attack, luckily that squad that past hadn't made it to the Seal and they were taking a level 5 so were heavily armed. After we took back the fort and helped clear the Office, I hooked up with reinforcements and we did a sweep of the area. Some on the initial fort defences were down but inside the Cathedral was much worse. Everyone inside was dead including Rune Master Marcus but they weren't cut, shot or chewed. Their eyes had been blown out of their sockets and were still smoking. I don't know if it was the blast or that guy, but whatever it was took them all out quickly and they didn't stand a chance. Not only that but the Pure gate was empty, no mist no aura just an arch of stones".

I turned back to the Commander waiting to see what she would say

"Thank you sergeant get yourself down to the mess hall and ..."

the sergeant cut her off

"sorry sir if it's all the same I want to go back out, two of my old squad went down today in the Cathedral and I don't want to be away from my duty if this isn't over". The Commander nodded and the Sergeant left the room. The Commander locked her hands together and softly said

"I am sorry, again gentlemen, the loss of anyone especially a the commander wentchild within our walls is a huge blow to all of us. I ..." just then the door burst open and a cadet ran in

"Commander I'm sorry you have to see this now it's urgent" we all rushed out with cadet to the main hall. The Commander gasped as we all looked up at the round circle on the wall, an imitation or mirror of the seal with all the lit up runes. Only it wasn't lit, all the seals where dark, except from the ninth and outer ring which were faint and barely glowing. She then rushed to the Command terminal where Major Williams was coordinating defences. The Commander went up to the Major "the seal has gone dark what does this mean? who is the next senior scribe? have any of our current teams reported back from their runs?" the Commander stared at the Major looking for information, The Major finished reading his clip board and answered

"We have lost communication with all current squads making their way to gates and reports are coming in across the globe that teams have disappeared, we are just waiting on updates from a team in Germany and Russia who have sent in a scouting team, their offices should be reporting to the citadel soon. The swarm of imps happened everywhere we've still had no word back from some offices I know one of the French and Greek teams are quiet" Just as the Major finished talking Scribe Jones walked into command, he was known for being a ponce as the number two scribe of the facility. Being suddenly promoted to number one had only raised his attitude problem

"Commander we need to raise the seal immediately, those teams aren't coming back" the Commander looked at him and began to scarlet

"and what do you suppose we do, leave them down there to

die" the scribe composed himself "Master Marcus had begun research into this 5 years ago after a dream he had, at first it was believed to be just a dream but one of the Israeli teams uncovered new scripture from the dead sea vaults that matched some of the images in his dream. Pertaining to the problem at hand I can tell you that the gates have been shut down. With none of the are gates active and we, are exceptionally vulnerable. Without the aura from those gates there is nothing to stop the bigger and most deadly of the demons surfacing and trying to break through" I butted in

"but the ninth gate why is it still glowing" the scribe looked at me like I'd just insulted his favourite slippers

"the ninth gate is for the most decrepit of sinners there hasn't been anyone through it in centuries chances are it is too far from the initial blast to have been knocked out" I was getting angry at this

"but it is still open so it can take souls"

"if you happen to have a level 9 to hand then by all means but the rest of us have work to do" and he walked off. The Commander still red but trying to sound sincere turned to James and I "boys go and be with your brothers and mother, Major Campbell see your family then as soon as your able please have your squads gathered anyone on their day off call them in. I want us prepared for any possible attacks, if this is the beginning of something then we will need to be ready" I looked at dad who was stone faced with anger over the attack and the callousness of the scribe, he nodded and said

"yes sir" and then gestured us out of the door.

# Chapter 9

## *A way in*

Mum, Lewis and Liam had been given an office room where we were to meet up with them, Lewis's body had been moved to another room and a cloth placed over him. Mum was holding the boys close, trying to keep herself calm when we were walking in the room. She looked up when we entered
"what's going on? why did this happen?" we were not sure how to answer this, thankfully dad walked in behind us just in time to explain "the honest answer is we don't know why it's started, but we don't think its ended either" he looked at Lewis and his face softened "hey son you ok?" he knew it was ridiculous but Lewis needed to hear dad talk normal and we weren't going to burst his bubble. James turned to dad "Dad, Ryan and I are going to see if there is anything we can do" dad looked at us "don't wander off, head along to your class and speak to your C/O but stay alert" we made our way to the academy, we really weren't sure what we planned to do, afterall we had only just graduated that day. As we were walking along we spotted the soul of an elderly lady talking to a member of the office team
"dearie I was supposed to be going to my gate today I was waiting for my husband but he hasn't arrived and I only have a couple of hours left, what's going on? Why aren't we going anywhere? What were those creatures?" the team-member tried desperately to explain teary eyed while doing so then the lady began fading away there and then, I couldn't believe my eyes and neither could the team-member. She stood up and looked bemused at us as though we might have an explanation

"she wasn't due for hours I don't understand I" she turned back around to where the old lady was then ran away to her offices before she began crying in the open, we kept walking so as not to draw too much attention. When we got into the class we saw a dozen or so of Finders from our year sitting on tables and chairs, Mia came up to James and hugged him,

"I'm so sorry" James hugged her then looked her in the eye

"it's ok he's with mum, dad and Liam just now" we explained to the group what we knew and everyone looked on in amazement, it was a few minutes before I asked where the LT was and Mia answered

"she told us to wait here until she had orders and headed out to the portal, supposedly they're shutting the seal." I began to think to myself, with the seal shut and the gates all down it doesn't look good for the souls. Arwa spoke up

"the Souls are going to be pilling in and fading away if that gate doesn't open" Mia shot Arwa a glare. James and I looked at each other and it just clicked

"it maybe sooner than we think, I don't think with the gates shut the souls can't stay in purgatory as long" my mind instantly rushed too Lewis we have to get him out of here, everyone sat talking to each other about what was going on and then Brian spoke

"Not all of the gate are closed" we all looked at Brian "The ninth gate is still active, kinda. Chloe and I have been thinking, remember the blast we got from the purity gate on our first trip, well Chloe read a log a few years ago about a team that took a level 4 through and accidently landed on level 5 the soul was through the gate before they noticed the level on the arch" James butted in

"but gates are specific to the soul" Chloe spoke up

"not necessarily its believed that the purer the souls the more gates are open, the further down you go. There has never been any reason to prove this as further levels are more dangerous. If we could get a pure soul through the gate maybe it could jump start the others" Simon less subtle jumped in "you see where they are going with this don't you". James and I looked at each other, is it an idea? or is it just suicide? either way we need to tell the Commander.

We wasted no time as we rushed to the command centre where scribe Jones was talking, James and I moved forward being stopped by the guards. James spoke up

"Please Commander we have to talk to you" The Commander beckoned us forward and we explained the theory before Jones jumped in "there has never been any research or accurately documented cases its reckless and there is nothing to suggest even possible" I got angry

"there is a case and it worked!" he postulated "a fluke at best, this office is for solutions not hunches" the Commander trying to keep her temper with the scribe sighed

"Begrudgingly, I have to side with Scribe Jones it's too dangerous and using your brother I'm surprised you're so willing to risk him in hell, to make the trip it would be suicide for even our most experienced teams at a time we can't afford to lose a single soldier. I'm sorry but that's my final word" we tried to stand our ground but were escorted out of the room.

We headed back to the class room to await orders from the LT, I kicked a chair and slumped into the one beside it. James walked up to the group

"still no word from the LT?"

"I guess with all the commotion we've been forgotten about" said Mia. Just as he went to sit down the door to the classroom opened, My head was down awaiting some patrol order at the back of the office

"so what's your plan batman" I know that voice anywhere

"grandad?" he chuckled a little but it sounded hollow

"came soon as I could. Overheard you boys speaking to the boss, I like the plan but it seems you've given up already?" he look at us expectantly

"what are we supposed to do?" Grandad took a seat next to us and leaned forward

"anyone here ever figure out why your dad is such a legend here yet? He was the most reckless cadet the academy had seen, but he was also one of the bravest. Just before graduation he was on a run, he had shown good fighting skills so they let him in on a level three run early on. The drop off had gone well five souls had made it no problem, but on the way back they were set upon by a golem. Not the loin cloth two voices kind, this was a being of rock and stone smashing its way around a chamber. In one strike it crushed two Finders breaking them killing them outright. It went for a third when your dad drew up his shield and shoulder barged it in to the wall. He dug his sword into the creatures shoulder and levered the arm away before it swung round and smacked him across the room. Your dad stood back up and the creature charged at him, just as it was about to crush him against the wall your dad rolled away holding his sword out sure and strong. He lunged forward and dug it deep where the leg would join causing the creature to tumble and smash against a sharp rock sticking out of the wall. Your dad's armour begins to glow bright white and sparks are coming off the metal, the creature looks up at your dad and gets one last look as he rammed his sword down the creature's throat. Cutting clean in two that one piece of life and flesh that makes you remember those abominations were once human. They carried the two dead back topside, being guided by your dad's armour still glowing with raw power and warding off all other creatures. Your dad was made Captain that next year and flew through the ranks earning the respect of any one in his command. The Finders he saved, one was the current Commander and the other, was your mother. It was his love for your mother that gave him the strength to take down a creature no-one had seen in centuries. Your little brother doesn't have a lot of time, I know you love him dearly and you have each other. Our family when we need to has always been able to summon our courage and strength when we needed it, something tells me we need it now more than ever. Your dad is going to be commanding the defences I will tell him what he needs to do but right now we need to get you someplace you can cause some mischief". I looked at James then at everyone in the room

"no-one has to come, but those who want to, pack well and for a fight, it's not going to be easy".

I took about 15 minutes to get my head together, 30 minutes to pack and 30 seconds to empty my bladder because I was shitting myself. Nine levels of hell, James was obviously coming and leader of the group, Brian and Simon didn't even give me a chance to answer. Chloe, Sarah and Steven hesitated but geared up and a few others got their armour on. Dixon and James were asked to run distraction so that our presence wasn't missed. James tried to tell Mia she wasn't coming but the threat of a broken wrist and castration swayed him. We gather back at the classroom taking an inventory, James got their attention

"last chance, this could be suicide, no way everyone gets out of this alive" no one backed down, grandad walked back in to the room

"I have organised our passage to hell but the seal is heavily guarded and the town has been locked down, any suggestions?"

Chloe was the first to answer

"the imps" Grandad looked at her

"I'm sorry"

"the imps they tunnel through preferring areas where trees grow in our world, with the swarm that we had earlier they are bound to have made a lot of larger than normal tunnels not big enough for the other creatures of hell to crawl up, but big enough for us to try and find a way down into the first level" grandad looked on impressed

"I like her, you must be Chloe, Brian has mentioned you" Brian looked bashful as grandad winks at him and Chloe struggles to remove the beaming smile on her face. Grandad paused for a second "I'm going out onto the battlements I maybe retired but I can still aim true, Brian you come with me to keep communication open, and keep me from falling off the roof" Brian looked at me and I nodded , I'd feel better knowing Brian was watching Grandads back, Arwa took the Gauntlet off her arm and handed it to Brian who put it in his pack. James and I went to go get

Lewis, he was still in the room with mum and Liam. Mum had been explaining to Lewis that he needs to go on a trip and that he would see all our old dogs and grandma would be there, she did also break it to him that the road was going to be scary, but as long as he stuck close to his brothers they would make sure he got there safe.

I didn't know if it was a trait unique to our family but every one of us reacted to bad news or loss differently to most families. Where many would still be wailing and inconsolable for hours even days, it was never long before we were joking around and ready to do whatever duty was required of us. News that stuff needed done or a tough road lay ahead didn't shake us we were ready for it all.

I looked at James and we knew that if the youngest of us can have the courage to move forward, we had better not let him down. I knew I would see my little brother to the gate, to whatever end may befall me. James took a knee to speak to Lewis

"Hey little brother, it's time we got a move on." Lewis looked at us and hugged Mum tightly who was supressing fresh tears

"I love you mum" he then hugged Liam "you can have my Lego and my scooter" Liam smiled at this and hugged his brother. Lewis looked at us "I'm ready James".

# Chapter 10

## *Level 1*
## The Plain and Mundane

I had to tell Lewis to go in a carry bag which he thought was great fun and be quiet which we knew would be the real challenge, but the wee guy didn't let us down. We grouped up in the main hall then made our way to the gate with Grandad following. He may be old or "seasoned" as he would say but seeing him and Brian with high powered rifles strapped to their backs just looked just awesome. We reached the departures gate and I stepped through the portal to hell, it was incredible in a few short hours the town looked like a military compound. Metal barricades had been set up all round the area, sniper nests where erected in the towers, RPGs, mortars and heavy machine gun nests in every position possible. Everyone was prepared for a fight, I asked grandad

"why doesn't it usually look like this?" he was looking all around himself

"because its hell, anything we build or set up begins to break down not in years but weeks we would never be able to keep it up. Not to mention this is the pure level, very few threats make it to the town let alone having ever breached into purgatory. Anyway this is where we part ways best of luck and be back by dinner" He winked at me and walked away with Brian towards the newly erected battlements choosing a tall tower above what would be the pub. Just as we were about to start making our way out the reinforced gate LT Williams stopped us in our tracks

"you lot are supposed to be in the class awaiting my orders

where the hell do you think you're going" I hadn't thought up an answer and she could take us all if we tried to force her hand, but I didn't have to

"they are under my orders Lieutenant " dad walked over

"Major Campbell Sir, may I ask what their mission is?" he looked at me and back at the LT "yes of course, I have tasked them to scout the breach point of the imps, I want that area locked down and cleared" the Lt looked back at us

"so many and heavily armed?" dad bared down at her

"today, I wouldn't accept anything less" the LT backed down straight away

"yes sir" and walked away. Dad put his arm on James's shoulder "look after them don't take un-necessary risks and make us proud, good luck. Oh and Chloe please keep Brian up to date I've given my gauntlet to Major Williams" he then whispers towards the pack "I love you Lewis be safe" he holds a tear before smiling at us and shouting the guards to open the main gate.

Steven led the way from the fortress, he could track better than any of us and sure enough the trail led to the town park where there would be a giant oak sticking out the ground.

"that's a lot of holes" Simon said as he started circling around the biggest one

"dude what makes you think we can get through from here?" James let Lewis out of the bag and stood up

"all routes underground are interlinked, it's like an ant farm" Simon looked down the hole

"so who's first?" we stared at him

"for fuck sake why is it always me" Mia was the first to answer

"you have got the biggest mouth, if it's safe to come down we can all hear you" This got a chuckle and even Simon smiled. James looked at everyone

"leave guns up here we don't want to be accidentally attracting unwanted attention with noise" the group looked at each other and then reluctantly removed all guns placing them in the duffle bag and laying it next to the oak tree. Simon sighed then gave a poor man's salute and jumped down. It wasn't long before we heard him

"Aw man an Imp turd!" I looked at James

"I guess it's safe" we sent down a few of the privates to help secure the level below, I went down followed by Lewis and James the rest followed. Sure enough a dirt slide with claw marks where the imps had been digging their way up, I had the ultimate wedgy. Mia was less subtle about hers

"my next shit is gonna be a clay urn that rode right up me arse" I couldn't help but give a laugh and I wasn't alone. James butted in "guard up and mouths shut, we are now below the seal and without the auras this can go bad fast. Steven and Simon take point I want diamond formation, Lewis is the priority protect at all cost, Mia please take three and guard the rear Ryan you stay close to Lewis" James gets down on one knee to Lewis "stay close to Ryan and do what he tells you and we will be out this nasty place before you know it. Everyone else stay in formation and keep your heads on a swivel" James give Lewis a wink and smiles at me. I know it is supposed to be a sign of trust, but I can't help but feel belittled and angry at being the babysitter. I don't know why I felt this way, James has a good plan and I want to look after Lewis. He is also the C.O. alongside Mia who let him take charge in the field. One of the privates piped up

"why aren't we using the Enigma Gauntlet to find our route?" Chloe turns to him

"because Lewis is pure if I track his gate we will find ourselves walking backwards, we're just going to have to find a route down and avoid the arterial lanes where we can". It wasn't long before we were on a descending track. Lewis's soul made our silver glow, but not as brightly as usual so tripping was all too easy. After a couple of hours the tunnel got bigger until we reached an open chamber, Simon paused

"well this is new" The chamber was large, walled with white sandstone tiles and Greek style pillars. The floor was large white slabs roughly cut. Flames torches were mounted on the pillars flickering a blue flame which gave the room an infrared hue. The smell of lavender and honeysuckle filled the air calming everyone nerves. Translucent figures were walking around randomly not speaking to each other, but speaking to the walls and themselves "ghosts? what are they doing?" said Gregson, James walks in

"looks like they are playing out events in their lives, Dante wrote that the first level was people living out a plain or mundane existence" I looked at him

"someone has been paying attention, you don't think there's going to be more of this do you?" James looked back disheartedly

"let us pray he was just a story teller little brother, or this trip is about to get a whole lot more interesting" We make our way past the spirits, some were having conversations often muttering then changing direction and beginning a new conversations. Others were doing tasks like knitting, filling out forms or kicking a tin can. One man looked like he was petting an invisible cat which looked a lot more un-nerving as it felt like he was staring right at us. I held Lewis close to me as we kept walking. Further and further we walked past these shadows as they lived out what we imagined was their former lives, Lewis laughed as a man on an invisible rowing machine who went faster and faster getting nowhere. I thought I recognised one of the ghosts from a soul I saw in purgatory a few months ago. We were walking for a while towards what we hoped was the exit before we heard Steven shout

"Peters keep away from them" but Peters kept walking towards one of the ghosts as though enthralled, I could hear a subtle ringing growing in my ears that I couldn't place and felt myself wanting to sheath my sword. Mia walked over to Peters and looked

"shit it's a siren everyone cover each other and don't listen to what they are telling you" the ghost leapt to grab Peters but not before Mia thrust her spear forward and the ghost went up in a puff of mist on the silver tip, Mia shouted "they may not feel pain but they still don't like silver everyone weapons up and let's get out of the chamber" we formed a moving hedgehog moving slowly towards the other side of the chamber. Ghosts from the edge of the room started floating towards us and making a grab for us, but we just kept swiping them away as we made it through. Half a dozen of what we suppose were ghosts, turned into wailing phantoms with glowing eyes forcing the other ghosts around to attack us and screeching a piercing screech as we kept moving. As we reached the end James cut down a rugby player charging towards him then the whole horde of spirits just disappeared.

"what the hell was that?" I asked

"the mundane" said James "the sirens would hold you in the chamber in their thrall until they had leeched all life from you and you joined the other spirits. Peters thanked Mia and we took one last look at the now empty chamber before moving forward. The chamber narrowed and we could see the light in distance behind us get dimmer, as we walked forward we could feel vibrations all around us and a low drone began in the back ground. As the pebbles around us lightly jumped about I tried not to imagine what was causing this. Instead I took some chocolate out of my pack, I offered a piece to Lewis forgetting he doesn't feel hunger or taste food, "no I'm ok thank you" Poor little guy, that felt mean for asking and I chose not to bite down on a piece in front of him

# Chapter 11

## Level 2
### Jormungandr

Moving through the tunnels we noticed the shape of the walls began to curve more and more, a light breeze began to whistle past us. One of the privates spoke up

"I thought there was no wind in the tunnels?" Chloe answered him

"there isn't, in Dante's second level he mentions wind pushing people back and forth, I imagine this is going to get stronger and make our journey that bit more difficult." Mia spoke up "that's one version, there is another" before she could finish a larger rumble began all round which grew stronger and stronger, earth began to crumble all about us and dust kicked up, we could hear something in the distance behind us. The noise grew louder and the earth shook even more violently by the minute, we were sure the tunnel was going to cave all around us. I grabbed Lewis and held him close to me as James shouted

"brace your selves against the walls, Lewis stay with Ryan!" It went on for ten minutes, a massive earth quake and an almighty growl before we heard a crash and the rumbling was over. We got to our feet looking around us, James took a visual inventory and roll call "any one hurt? Check each other and your weapons I don't want anyone caught out if this goes sideways" he is always the cautious one and knows what to lookout for. One of the private's sheaths his weapon and turns to James

"what the hell was that?" James sheaths his sword and answers back looking at the ceiling

"I don't know, but whatever is was made its way to the surface and without the seals active on the plate I'm guessing it made it through with little effort, if it did then the route behind us before long, is going to be full of creatures and demons clambering for the surface. We can't go back, getting those seals active again maybe the only hope the surface, souls and the world have". James used to be the quiet one but hearing him give this speech, even I felt ready to rally up and charge forward. It wasn't long before we were on the march again, with the newly opened hole behind us we could feel wind rushing past us faster and faster. Walking on we came to another large chamber that opened up and finding our footing became even more difficult. Chloe tripped over a pile on the floor

"what the hell is this" Mia paused and peered down then gasped "snake skin" she bent down for an even closer inspection and I could see a worst fear stricken on her face

"this is the world snake Jormungandr from Norse mythology, this is very bad news" James looked at her and signalled the group to a small cove, he organised the troops into defensive positions and gathered Myself, Simon, Chloe and Mia close by. Steven was the most alert of the team and was asked to scout but stay close. James huddled us close

"right, Yogun I need to know everything" Mia looked at Chloe for support before speaking

"in the legend he is the child of Loki and attacks during Ragnarock. He was a serpent so large he could crush the world but is killed by Thor. But not before biting Thor and poisoning him, after nine steps Thor died." Chloe looked at her and we all pondered the legend before Simon spoke "well I don't think it's THAT big" we all looked at him and James spoke

"no the legends and reality are going to have some discrepancies but there are a few things we can take from it" Simon looked disparagingly "like what?" James gave a look to say shut up, keep your voice down and listen "we know it's a snake therefore this wind is going to be messing with its cold blood, it's probably trying to hide from it. If we stay in the cold spots and away from open passage ways we may be able to slip by undetected and uncoiled" This didn't settle Simon

"anything else?"

"Yes if Thor did injure or banish the snake then it has a weakness, you'll just have to avoid the fangs Simon" James smirked at a now grumpy Simon. James grouped everyone else round and gave them a brief on the plan and how we were going to get through, one of the privates did drop 3 shades but everyone was ready to press on. Lewis was the one that seemed to give everyone strength not flinching at all when we said there was a monster lurking nearby. He just looked up at me saying

"it's cool Ryan can take it" smiling at me and me back at him. We made our way forward climbing over the dead skin trying to stay in the winds path, we felt the cold air whistling through our armour and it made us all feel the chill. The armour wasn't really made to keep out the cold as we didn't come across it often in our line of work, so holding our cloaks tightly round us was our only real defence. We knew from our studies that Lewis would be fine, temperature didn't have any effect on souls but the wind did make it difficult for him to grasp so I tied a rope around him and me.

As we reached the midpoint of the chamber the wind seemed at its strongest, it felt like we were stupidly forcing your way into a tornado, forcing us to sheath all weapons and fight to keep our balance. My eyes were watering as I looked up fighting to see ahead, then with no warning as I climbed over the next rock feeling for a grip, the wind just died. Simon was the first to speak "What just happened?" I looked around frantically for a sign of what had stopped the wind, all my senses were tingling with the sensation of the wind stopping and then we heard it. That slimy serpent slither began creeping along coming out of a tunnel. It took no time at all and the snake began to slither around the rocks about and us enclosing us in

"group up, Lewis in the middle we don't want to be separated this thing can hunt us out with little effort". It sounded as though it was just going round in circles toying with us, all I could see was the huge body coloured a brilliant red with black patches racing around us in circles. All of a sudden it stopped and we waited in tense silence. Then the rocks began to break and crush around us, it wasn't toying it was coiling in an attempt to crush us all at once "climb! CLIMB!" there was a rock spire near us we scrambled for it and I threw Lewis up to James, I got up just as one of the privates tripped running to another rock nearby. The snakes head in a flash leapt over its own coils and snatched him up in the blink of an eye then retreated behind its scaled wall. We didn't even hear him scream the monster was so fast, we began firing arrows at the skin but they just ricochet off "find the weak spot!" I heard James call and I look all around me trying to spot one but all I could think was somewhere in these coils one of my friends was gone. The rocks were still breaking around us and crumbling to dust, the snake lifted its head slipping its serpent tongue in and out trying to get a look at us and we spot our mark, one eye peered at us a black marble reflecting the light from our amour, but one of the snakes eyes was glazed and the snake tilted its head slightly to the left to gaze at us gauging what kind of threat we posed. It didn't seem fazed perhaps thought we were meagre morsels compared to the feed it was really after. It lunged at the rock we were perched on but we knew it was coming so we scrambled out of the way and the snake crashed nose first into the rock. We used this moment of confusion to try and hide amongst the remaining rocks around us, the inner rocks were thicker and these proved too strong for the snake to crush, but it was still making a persistent effort. We were in the inner circle and we were trapped, we all looked at James who was rapidly thinking up a plan on what to do. It didn't take long as he began to use hand signs to signal us "Simon you're the bait the rest of us will try to draw its attention but you will be its main target" Simon was the fastest and I'm guessing his free running was felt to be the most apt skill in this situation. "Mia and I will climb the spire again, Steven and Peters flank round with flares as soon as it spots Simon. Throw them where Simon is going, it will throw off the snakes judgement long enough for us to get into position" I gestured to him

"what about me?" and he pointed straight at Lewis I knew fine what I needed to do. I knew how important it was but still begrudged the duty but I pulled Lewis close to me and kept cover. "On my mark, NOW!" the troops began firing arrows and creating as much noise as possible while maintaining their cover. Simon then began leaping from rock to rock like a rubber ball fired from a cannon, the snake spotted him immediately and began to take aim swaying with the rhythm of Simons movements. It was about to strike when Peters and Steven began to throw flares in Simon's direction creating this phosphorus bright trail leading towards the spire, the snake not being deterred took a lunge at Simon. The snake came crashing down and Simon feeling its presence leapt out of the way and the snake missed crashing into another rock. It did not recover quite so quickly as the first time as it lay still on the ground dazed. James and Mia leapt down from the spire crashing a sword into one eye and a spear into the other. It whimpered, slithered and then fell silent. We all emerged from our hiding spots and stared at it as it lay there, its coils loose now on the rocks around us that it was trying to crush.

"That! was too fucking close!" Simon was panting leaning against the spire holding his chest. Chloe stepped forward and took an empty vial out of her pouch, Mia looked at her curiously and Chloe spotted her bemusement "What? This stuff killed Thor you never know when something like this could come in handy" Chloe raised the mouth of the serpent and used a wire to crush a secondary fang that dripped what we guessed was the elusive poison that killed Thor. No-one else dared to stick their hands into the mouth of the creature, instead we gathered our gear and began to head for the other end of the chamber. As we got to the exit the wind began to pick up a little but in the opposite direction, it was pushing us forward almost like it was beckoning us to leave.

Once we had gone down the passage a few feet James stopped and turned around to look at us all "we know that this road is not going to be easy and I don't blame anyone who wants to go back, we will mourn our dead when we return, until then we do what we do best and look after each other. Stick together, keep each other safe and destroy anything that gets in our way". He was right, the time to mourn would have to wait.

We all continued forward without hesitation trying not to think about the one we lost. That was until we came across one of the teams that had been down in the tunnels when the swarm hit us. We looked at the mangled and torn bodies surrounded by dead imps, the soldiers bore scratch marks all over and we know they put up a hell of a fight before receiving deep bites in their necks and arteries. We guessed they were in the tunnel when the imps swarmed and any attempt to fight back was futile but they would have fought to the last breath. We checked for pulses but there was no need, too much blood lay for anyone to be alive and the souls weren't to be found. Maybe they had completed their mission before they died, maybe they didn't. We didn't have a choice either, we had to complete our mission or lose everything.

# Chapter 12

## The Breach
### (The Fort)

"So you and Chloe are getting quite serious then?" Grandad grinded at Brian as they stood on the battlements adjusting their scopes and placing their back-up magazines in easy to reach spots. Brian tried to pretend like he hadn't heard him "she's a nice girl, very clever" he grinned again and looked over at Brian who was trying to maintain his gaze on a rotten tree stump near the Seal "yes she reminds me of my wife, amazing woman she could wield Sai blades better than anyone I knew" Brian looked up

"Sai Blades?" Grandad knew he had his attention now

"yes three pronged dagger usually dual wielded, she could cut down 10 imps 5 hounds and a Demon in the blink of an eye without breaking a sweat. Course she couldn't cut toast with quite the same finesse, woman couldn't cook at all actually, but that's not why I married her" Brian giving into the conversation looked at him

"why was it then?" Grandad laughed

"because she made me a better fighter, a better leader and if you don't mind me saying a very satisfied happy man" Brian tried not to think about this

"your point?" Grandad face became more stern "my point is simple lad, when she gets back up here tell her you Love her. Ryan said your still playing hard to get around her even though your already together" Brian had heard enough "thanks for the pep talk, but let's focus shall we" Grandad chuckled

"yes, yes have it your way but before long you'll be wanting to message her just to make sure she's ok" Brian tried to keep his focus on the stump but wasn't really focusing on it and grandad could see it.

As Brian was looking forward failing to maintain his concentration, the earth around them began to rumble and crack. They could hear and feel it getting louder and louder closer with every second. Major Williams who had come out to the battlements once he had given all the orders he could indoors, began to shout

"battle stations all safety's off", The noise was becoming unbearable as more and more pebbles began bouncing like they were on an invisible subwoofer. Then what sounded like banging vibrated through the air and ground until the seal, chains and all were launched in the air and came crashing down the sound ricocheting off the landscape. It sounded like a large bell being dropped and bellowing out to the heavens. A huge demon 50 ft high emerged engulfed in flames. It looked like a giant skeleton of a huge ogre like monster bellowing orange flame from its centre and all around. Major Williams was shouting once again "It's a behemoth! Mortars, load explosive silver nitrate, orientate 45 degrees, south 2 clicks and fire for effect on my signal. The creature was barely out of the hole when the order came. "Team 1 FIRE!, Team 2 FIRE!" several projectiles hurtled towards the monster then came crashing into it exploding, sending molten bone everywhere and splintering the creatures skull. The monster went down with a mighty crash and the flame that once burned brightly fizzled out leaving a huge pile of cindered bones that began collapsing into the open pit. The fort erupted with cheer at the creature's quick destruction. Major Williams shouted over the cheers "Don't let your guard down that creature was nothing more than a big can opener, be at your ready".

Major Williams told his assistant to go to the Office and pass on orders to close the main gate to the portal. We couldn't shut down the portal but we could roll 2 tonnes of steel in front of it which was better than nothing. The assistant wasted no time clutching the orders tight in his grip then running towards Purgatory as more and more troops were marching in to hell and setting up positions. An offensive group of troops was being formed in the main square all armed with swords, spears and shields.

Commander Mcmail read the orders nodded to the messenger and gave the order immediately "close the gate, begin the lock down, have all remaining troops stationed in defensive positions at the departure gate". On the tannoy system announcements were made "all remaining security personnel to the gate, lock down is in effect. All souls please head to the main auditorium. The Commander was starting to get impatient with her new lead scholar "what have you found out? How has this happened and how the hell can we fix it?" the scholar sensing her impatience was fumbling for answers only to say that his team was working on it. The Commanders anger continued to rise "and the ninth gate what about that? is it being considered?" This flustered Jones, he spread his hand in an attempt to emphasis his argument "it isn't Sir, there's no way for it to work" The Commander growled

"so far it's the closest anyone has come to an answer, now get a move on" Master Jones left the room not daring to utter a syllable retort.

Brian counted off magazines and grandad set up a 50cal sniper rifle between them lifting a magazine and looking at Brian

"these are explosive armour piercing rounds, use sparingly and be careful of the kick back" Patting the rifle he looks up "lets pray we don't need her eh" Grandad then handed Brian a piece of chalk, Brian looked at it

"what the hell is this for?" Grandad laughed "keeping score, you might be as good as me on the range son, but I've been looking forward to an opportunity like this" Brian couldn't help but grin at this placing the chalk next to his perch "you're on Popps what are we playing for?" Grandad thought about it

"Bragging rights obviously, but I suppose we can play for drinks, larger the lead more drinks to be bought by the looser" Brian nodded

"you are on" and the game was on, Brian had been wanting to settle this argument too. All they needed now was their targets and they wouldn't have to wait long.

# Chapter 13

## Level 3
### Hot breath

Steven took point and decided to scout ahead with two privates using the oil burners for light, the rest of us had a rest and trailed behind

"so is this going to be the thing?" Simon said as he scanned the tunnel markings

"Probably" said James in answer back "Murphy's law" said Chloe, Simon screwed up his face

"what's that?"

"it states that anything that can go wrong, will go wrong so you might as well just brace and get on with it" Simon pondered this and shrugged

"I only ever heard of Cole's Law" Chloe looked puzzled

"what's that?"

"Salad, mayonnaise, some carrot, lettuce, whatever you feel really" the sigh could be felt all round I tried not to laugh but he did make me smile

"You do, do my head in sometimes you idiot" Just then we heard a yell and moments later footsteps running towards us, we raised our weapons but only Steven and one other appeared

"where is Gregson?" James asked trying to see further down the tunnel as though Gregson would be just behind. Steven was shaking his head and took a minute to catch his breath. He leaned up against the tunnel wall and started pointing back down the tunnel shaking his head more. Through exhausted breath he spoke

"we got to a set of tunnels up ahead, we think they all intersect into the main chamber. We took one and followed it down then came across a couple of hell hounds sleeping, we took them out all stealthy you know easy enough and decided to scout the main chamber. Everything looked ok and we could see the black stone arch exit, Gregson lit a flare and held it high so we could get a better view. It was then we felt a hot breath over our shoulders, huge teeth were glaring down on us, I managed to get an arrow off which caused the beast to flinch so we could get away and run down a tunnel that it was too big for. Philips and I made it down but it caught Gregson by the leg and before I could lose another arrow" Steven took a deep breath

"he was pulled back and the other head ripped him in two, there was nothing we could do so we ran with that thing banging and clawing where we left. A couple of hounds chased us but we got rid of them" Steven slumped down wiping his brow on his sleeve. Mia put her hand on his shoulder

"what do you mean the other head? what was it?" Steven looked up wiping more sweat from his brow

"for my money, Cerberus" I looked at James who knew instantly "Greek mythology, massive three headed guard dog of hell. Level three was either going to be him or a giant worm, not sure which one I hoped for least"

Simon walks up and down the tunnel

"ok so how do we take on a three headed dog, I'm guessing not by sneaking past it and you can go to … well hell if you think I'm scratching it behind the ear". James thinks about this as he passes and talks to himself out loud

"It can hear us and smell us, a dogs weakest point is its nose and this has three of them" Chloe felt stupid but said her idea anyway "don't suppose fetch would work?" Simon responded quickly to this

"count me out, the bait doesn't usually dangle twice and live to talk about it" I smiled and mocked

"quality of the catch is in the bait mate" I wink at him as he is now scowling at me. James continues to think out loud

"In the legend Hercules uses his giant club, but beating down three heads single handed is either very skilled or not how it went down" he paused and turned to Steven "Steven what obstacles or cover did you see in the chamber?" Steven thinks about this

"I didn't see anything we could hide behind, but the tunnels all seemed linked like an outer ring, except one which I'm guessing is the exit it. It's a stone arch and I did spot that it has some runes on it" Chloe buts in

"what runes did you see?"

"I didn't get a great look but saw a fork with a dot, a harp or lute of some kind and a sickle. I didn't recognise the rest." Chloe took a moment to process everything before James spoke

"have you got anything?"

"The first symbol is Hades it's shown on our seal obviously a reference to the dogs master, the sickle I'm not sure could be one of many things in Greek or other mythology, but the lute. The lute is a basic symbol it represents music, in the tales Orpheus uses music to put Cerberus to sleep before entering the underworld" Mia stands up

"are you serious? Music? this thing might as well be trained by Hagrid" This got a few laughs before Chloe spoke

"yes, same idea but seeing as we haven't exactly brought along any instruments I think you, will be perfect for the job" Chloe stands pointing at Mia and everyone stares at Mia "why me?" she says sounding confused and insecure (for the first time ever) Chloe walked towards her

"Sandys bar, June 13th Karaoke night, ring any bells?" Mia shook her head worried hoping Chloe would drop it "you can sing Mia and very, very well" We all looked at each other a little bemused before I had to ask

"what song did she sing?" Mia not happy this was divulged lost her cool

"NONE OF YOUR BUSINESS!" snapping at me then back round. Chloe spoke softly to her

"if you have got a better idea I'm all ears, but there is no need to snap" Mia bowed her head a little

"Evanescence, My immortal" she muttered. James spoke before any of the rest of us asked her to repeat herself

"It's the best plan we've got" he moved closer to Mia to talk quietly "she's not wrong, you can sing and we need a route through. Those tunnels should carry the sound allowing us to make our escape" Mia nodded reluctantly but remained a shade of scarlet that could only be rivalled by her hair.

We made our way along the tunnel when Steven got us all to pause and whispered to James

"here is the best spot any further in and we might as well ring the dinner bell" James got us all close to give out our orders

"right everyone follow Steven to the entrance closest to the exit. Mia, Simon and I will go to the other side and begin the diversion. Once the dog is out, look for one of Simons daggers and try not to get impaled." He turned to me and I answered

"yeah, yeah keep Lewis safe and with me" He nodded but I wasn't looking at him. A red mist came over my eyes again, fucking babysitting duty again why does he get to play hero for Mia and I'm stuck back here what makes him so special

"hess not, you areee" What? No, I shook my head looking around me for the voice and reassured myself it was nothing, this isn't me I don't think like this. I tried to shake off the horrible feeling but that voice seemed to be haunting me again and this horrible hatred of my brother began to grow again no matter how much I tried to ignore it.

James's voice came back into my head and I started to focus again

"everyone you know what to do, now stay quiet any I'll see you on the other side, wait for us there and we will be with you"

We started to make our way round to the other side, Steven reckoned it would take around twenty minutes of moving quietly to get us all round to the tunnel exit closest to the arch. We stayed low and crawled around the slew hell hounds that Steven killed when he first came in. We could hear Cerberus sniffing around, he had caught our sent but couldn't figure out where we were. Steven knew his craft well and we weren't about to question his steps, every time he put his arm up and told us to stop we did so immediately.

We eventually made it to the end tunnel and crouched down, it was about 10 minutes before it started. We could hear Cerberus moving back to the other side of the chamber and barking, the three heads creating a bellowing echo painful to listen to and he was pawing the ground looking for something. We could hear those massive claws tearing rubble and stone searching for its prey. We didn't believe the plan was going to work over this noise, but he then dropped to a growl and then to nothing, it became so quiet not even his steps could be heard. Then a voice, soft and gentle began to grow louder and louder over the hot breath of the hound. The tunnels began to carry the sound all round us and before we knew it, we were being enveloped in some of the most soothing and beautiful music I have ever heard.

"...When you cried, I'd wipe away all of your tears, when you'd scream, I'd fight away all of your fears..."

None of us could move, we just knelt there listening and forgetting why we were even there. The red earth and crushing walls of hell just, melted away around us. The music carried so well around the chamber that a soft vibration pulsed off my skin with each note, I closed my eyes and pictured the silhouette of a woman singing her child off to sleep. I was so at peace nothing could unsettle me, that was until a whistling could be heard through the air and a silver knife came hurtling through the chamber and embedded into the wall beside us. We moved swiftly and quietly as we all went into the tunnel leading out once we were at least 100yds down from the arch we settled down and awaited the others. We were too far to hear the music and we guessed by now it had stopped, 45 minutes passed and we waited but they didn't appear. Steven offered to scout back but I asked him to stay with Lewis while I did it. I got to the chamber exit and looked across but I could barely see, I raised my lantern but I couldn't see anyone around. Don't know what went through my head but I started calling for them in a strange shout whisper

"James? Simon? Mia?" nothing I tried again but still no sound returned. Then I heard a loud grunt and the lifting of a huge body as the hound shook its enormous heads shaking off its slumber. The dog had woken back up and it began sniffing around the other side of the cavern. I started to get a cold sweat and wasn't moving, then I heard James shout

"GET IN YOU PILLOCK" Simon leaped and tackled me back into the tunnel followed by James and Mia charging in behind just before the dog tackled the stone arch barely missing them, we tumbled down re-gained out footing then scrambled down the tunnel to the others, the sound of the dog clawing at the tunnel fading into the distance. Once we had joined the others and caught our breath James grabbed me and squared up to me "you fucking idiot what were you thinking? I told you to wait with Lewis we could have died you almost ruined the entire plan!" he let me go staring at me, I didn't know what to say, a stammering excuse left my lips

"you've been gone for ages we thought something had happened to you" Mia was angry again and weighed in

"BIG dog, dark tunnel, can't sing while sneaking needed to be quiet and didn't want to chance it. Did you need a fucking degree to figure all that out?" as she walked past me James joining her, Simon came walking close behind them

"don't look at me dude she has a point, I'm still in one piece though and that was a sweet tackle" He patted me on the shoulder and walked on. I met back up with Lewis and we all started walking, me with my head in my chest as I kept thinking everyone's eyes were looking at me. Lewis called up to Mia

"you have a nice voice Mia" She gave a forced smile

"thank you Lewis" I felt her smile drop and daggered gaze on me.

# Chapter 14

## First Wave
### (The Fort)

Grandad was humming away to himself merrily as Nine thousand men and woman trained their eyes on the crater that once held the Great Seal. Tensions were high as everyone awaited the impending attack. Another rumble began and everyone knew their wait was over, it was coming. Fingers were hovering over triggers waiting for the order to fire, the earth shook pebbles all around once more. Without warning great boulders began hurtling out of the hole and landing just short of the opening. Major Williams shouted

"hold your fire" Brian turned to Grandad

"hold fire? They're giving themselves defences to hide behind" Grandad looks at Brian but hints towards his scope. Thirty or so boulders landed at different points but still so sign of the combatants though the rumble did not stop, then a great roar could be heard all round piercing into the sky turning it a blood red, red lightning began forking in the distance lighting up the sky. Soldiers determined not to be swayed stayed focused on the seal so as not to give into fear. Major Campbell my Dad could now be heard

"you are the guardians of the dead, you are the last defence of the living, we are the Pathfinders, we are the greatest warriors the world has ever known, if hell is what they want! We. Will. GIVE. THEM. HELL!" cheers erupted all around and everyone rallied ready to defend the fort. At that moment a shadow appeared in the distance upon the horizon. Grandad turned to Brian "well I guess it was too much to ask that they would all come out of the one hole if they can dig elsewhere, at least they can't dig near the fort" Brian looks at him "old magic my boy always be ready" Grandad grinned and started looking around to take aim on the best target he could "remember lad I like the finest Jamesons" he grinned ear to ear to himself.

The black cloud became bigger and bigger Major Williams shouted again

"artillery take aim and fire on my command everyone else, you know what to do, this fort does not fall".

# Chapter 15

## Level 4
### Sisyphus

"Does anyone else feel like the tunnels down here are all a bit, I don't know, empty?" Simon said while stumbling on a rock. James very stoic answers

"if they aren't here then we can only assume that they are making their way topside and making things difficult for everyone else. Still, don't let your guard down lets avoid as many surprises as possible". One of the privates began to grumble

"Sir it's been hours can we take a rest please" I was about to give him a line about the enemy not resting and the fate of the world at stake when James spoke

"go ahead if the last few tunnels are anything to go by then the next chamber isn't far away and we are going to need all our strength, if the next challenge is anything like the last one at least" I wanted to argue but I bit my tongue. I was tired and getting some water and food right now sounded like a good idea, I sat down and bit into a protein bar then looked at my little brother

"sorry Lewis you want anything?" he just looked at me and I know it was stupid to ask him again but it felt normal to me, he just grinned and answered

"no I'm ok thanks, I'm not hungry and I'm getting use to the tunnels, it's like going into those spooky haunted houses at the shows" I smiled

"I guess so, you always stayed close to me in those too" it was a lovely moment and it felt like nothing was wrong. Like he would be going back to school tomorrow with Liam and he would be waking me up as he always did before he left. I tried not to let it show, but I knew those were the stupid little moments I would miss the most when this was all over.

A salt air began to brush past us filling the tunnel with smells of the ocean, everyone breathed deep as the cool air rush was soothing and pleasant on the cheek. James looked back "Steven would you?" Steven nodded to James and he took one of the privates along with him to scout ahead, Private Foster was reluctant but Steven gave everyone confidence after seeing his skills in the last tunnel. The rest of us waited for them to return and we took this moment to get some more food and water down us. As we waited we also began to check our weapons and re pack our bags to make sure everything was secure, they were getting lighter. After fifteen to twenty minutes both returned quite casually, we all gave a sigh of relief

"no creatures this time by the look" Simon said as he swivels a knife in his hand "what did we get then?" Steven had a small grin as he spoke "boulders, lots and lots of boulders." Everyone looked at him confused

"so where is the sea air coming from?" I asked "no idea, up ahead it's a never ending run of 8 boulders, from 8 entrances, just rolling in 8 spirals and falling in synchronised sequences to a centre where they fall through " I looked at Steven

"why is that a reason to smile? We still have to get past giant boulders"

"yeah but they don't chase you with teeth" Private Gilbert snorted

"you've never seen raiders of the lost ark mate" a small chuckle was heard all round. James's patience still sounded tested

"gear up let's get going, sooner we get a move on, sooner we are out" We picked up our gear and started back on the tunnel not taking long to enter into the next chamber. We look around from the entrance and sure enough spotted a load of boulders, but they weren't the only things we saw

"they weren't there when we left?" Steven said as he walked forward to see more. The boulders weren't falling, they were being held up by souls, sometimes two or three attempting to push them back up the hill, we stared at them for a moment trying to figure out what we were looking at

"what are they doing?" I asked. Chloe who was ready with the answer spoke

"Sisyphus" she paused "he was once king of Corinth who tricked death into letting him live. When death finally took him he said you have a choice, stay in a basic plain of existence for eternity or if you manage to push the rock to the top you may go to Elysium, Greek heaven. Sisyphus took the deal and has been pushing the rock ever since along with others that death offered or tricked into this deal, some say it was actually Icarus that" I jumped in

"ok we get the idea so how do we get passed?" I sounded way more sarcastic than I meant too "easy Ryan" James snapped back, he was right why was I snapping at Chloe for no good reason and she looked angrily at me

"sorry" I muttered trying to sound sincere.

Simon was the first to the break silence

"are we waiting for them to drop the rocks or can we go?" James put his hand in front to stop anyone moving forward

"that's exactly what we are going to do" everyone paused " they do this for eternity right which means once they get to a certain spot they will drop the boulders and start again, when they do that we go in groups. If we all go then we will be tripping on each other's feet"

We watched as the spirits slow drudge came to an end and the boulders began their ballet decent into the black abyss. It was mesmerizing to watch as three more boulders from each exit came tumbling down with no sign of where they were from, or where they were going. We could see our exit on the other side, once again a black arch with runes beckoned us towards it. I gave my sword and pack to Simon being the fastest and put Lewis on my back, we waited patiently for James to give the order. First to go was Steven and two privates, they slipped a little but were soon clambering their way to the top before the ghosts disappeared and the ballet began again. Next it was Simon, Lewis and I. I could just make out the white glisten of the spirit closest to us appear before I heard "GO!" we leapt like hounds on a track and I could see the white rabbit I was chasing. We clambered along the 45 degree slope trying not to lose our footing "don't go too close to the pit" I could still hear James shouting but my focus was getting Lewis out of there. My hands were covered in soil as I kept picking myself up to keep moving forward, I didn't even notice anyone else around me as Lewis was my only goal. I scrambled up the slope under the arch and stopped in the tunnel with Lewis on my back, I lowered him down and just as my head lifted to see where the others were the boulders were tumbling again. James sent the rest in their groups and they each clambered to the top, I had never seen Mia run so fast. James, Chloe and Private Foster were last, just as they began and got to the centre I saw the spirit holding the rock in front of me look my way as though it was staring right at me, as though it warning me what was going to happen. Right before it disappeared the boulders began tumbling and I could see the others scrambling to get out of the way. Now I could barely make out anyone below as the boulders were descending faster and faster "there I see them" Mia pointed to a spot to the left less than 30 yards from the pit, James and Private Foster had one of Chloe's arms around a shoulder as one of her legs looked limp. They were desperately trying to get up the gravel as another boulder came hurtling towards them. James forced them to the right uphill just dodging it as it shot passed them. I looked over as Foster dodged left and down and slipped, he starting to slide towards the pit. He crawled with all his might but not before a boulder hurled into him knocking him out, rolling him and forcing him down the hole where he was gone. I winced slightly but was focused on making sure no one else went

"stay with Lewis" I shouted to Mia as I grabbed a rope and timed my sprint down to James, I barely missed one step before getting down to them

"what are you doing?!" James shouted

"what does it look like!" I threw Chloe the rope and tied it round myself

"you carry, ill pull" we started to get up pausing when we were about to be hit and moving out of the way, there was definitely more boulders falling this time than earlier. I was half way up the hill when Chloe slipped pulling us all backwards, in that moment I flailed trying to get upright. I could see the stone rolling towards me but I couldn't move fast enough and braced for the impact, but it never came. I uncrushed one eye and looked up to see a spirit holding the boulder trying to push it without even looking at me. I wasn't stopping to ask questions I got up checked the other two and then pulled them up to the arch. All three of us fell through the arch and breathed a sigh of relief

"what the hell were you thinking?" I thought I was hearing things but it was James shouting to me

"what? Saving your life clearly!" my brow narrow at him as he answered me pointing at Lewis

"you have one job, take care of Lewis. It doesn't matter about anything or anyone else, Lewis is your charge and that's an order" I couldn't believe it and snapped back

"your fucking welcome" James stormed off down the tunnel leaving the rest of us lying there as the spirits and boulders continued their dance. After a few minutes of silence Chloe shuffled over to me

"thank you" she smiled which after the way I snapped at her earlier I welcomed gladly

"that's oryt, how's your ankle?" she massaged it "just sprained I went over it trying to keep my footing, I thought I was going down that pit for sure" I smiled then thought about the lad who didn't make it, Wayne Foster I think his name was. Admittedly I didn't know him well but he was one of the crew, he had come in from Glasgow I think. Another loss hit us all and we sipped our water cans silently. Mia stood up "I'm going to make sure he's ok" and began walking down the tunnel to check on James.

The sea air began to hit me again and I sniffed it as though trying to find the source, I turned to Chloe sitting beside who was rubbing some ointment on her ankle Steven had given her. "any thoughts on the seas salt smell?" I said and Chloe lifted her head trying to hide the pain

"not really, only that the pitch fork rune on the arch back there. I thought it might have been Satan's pitchfork, but might actually be for Poseidon's trident" I laughed

"scrambling for our lives and you still managed to spot what symbols were on the door" she smiled wincing again

"you never know what will come in handy" she lowered her trouser ankle and began spinning up her Rune Gauntlet

"who you messaging?" As if I didn't know and she did go a little red at the question

"Just letting Brian and your dad know what's happened and what's going on, with any luck I may even get a reply soon too". Simon began singing to himself

"I got the moves like …..I got the moves like…." We all looked at him "what? Rolling stones, song just popped into my head". Another heavy sigh as we decided to get some water and rest. I Sat there looking at my water tank

"Conserve your rations guys, I wouldn't mind making it back" Everyone studied their rations and nodded.

# Chapter 16

## XXX
### (The Fort)

All at once the fortress erupted with the sound of gun fire in all directions as heavy gun emplacements cut down demon after demon that was hurtling towards the fort. A lieutenant was giving orders to the mortar teams that were raining silver shrapnel rounds upon an ever persistent enemy.

"45 north, 23 east fire on my word, NOW" a loud 'phutung' could be heard as the shell dropped down in the launcher and was then hurtled in the air towards its target. The machine guns were being fed by two men teams working in perfect synchronicity, the bullets flowing as fluid as water through a tap. Men and Women are on the walls holding assault rifles, picking off large targets and those attempting to flank the main fire. Brian and Popps along with all the other snipers in their nests, were moving from target to target calling out swarms in all directions only stopping to reload their magazines. Shot, shot, shot, shot, shot, shot, shot, shot, shot, shot, Reload, X, shot, shot... in 15 minutes both Brian and Popp had marked 3 X's on their patches of wall. 30 targets each dropped, enemies falling with no idea where the shot had come from and the demon beside them running with no idea they were next.

In the office updates from the field were coming in fast and the office scribes were translating messages as quick as possible "Main gate holding strong, artillery at 60%, heavy guns at 50% minimal casualties to our forces. Enemy forces heavy fatalities but reinforcements still approaching in greater numbers" The Commander looked at her next in command in the office a Colonel Hendricks. Hendricks was a rigid man with a deep voice African complexion and Queens English accent. He was co-ordinating the main room like a well-oiled machine, the Commander listening to the call outs looks at the Colonel

"how much longer can we hold out?" the Colonel considers his answer

"at present rate of use we have 6 hours of ammunition" he then looks at his charts "we have reserves just set to go out and restock ammo supplies, we will have the gate open no longer than 30 minutes, but once restocked if the flow of Demons stays at this constant we will have 10 hours give or take before hand to hand combat is our only option" A cold bead of sweat ran down the Commanders back, but she didn't break her composure as many looked up for her reaction.

"What news have we had from the other facilities?" the Colonel nods towards one of his staff who responds

"Sir we aren't getting much information but so far we have had heavy attacks on all American stations, European and Asian stations. Other continents have sporadic attacks but not as strong, we have lost word from 8 offices globally. The citadel is mobilising teams to check them out but with the current level of attack, it could be hours before they can do anything or we hear anything"

The Commander put her hands on the metal railing in front of her and bows her head contemplating the magnitude of the attack "these things have been crawling underground like cockroaches gathering their forces waiting for this day, but how is there so many? How have they gone undetected so easily and why is today special?" she looks out the office towards the Scholar annex but there was no sign of anyone coming to give her news.

"Have we heard anything from the detention level? Have they got any answers?" another officer answered

"No Sir nothing yet" she shook her head trying to think of her next move thinking to herself, can we get a team down there? could it reboot the gates? she called out to her guards "have the Campbell twins brought in here and that Chloe girl" one of her guards nodded and walked away to get them.

# Chapter 17

*Level 5*
**Without a Paddle**

We got to our feet and were beginning to feel the weight of walking upon the soles of our boots, even though our packs were getting lighter. I stood up then helped Lewis to his feet, a small smile was spread across his face

"what's with the cheesy grin?" he looked at me and it grew, we started walking down the tunnel towards where we guessed Mia and James were whilst the others gathered themselves. Lewis was strolling lightly talking away

"I remember that three day hiking holiday we went on with dad, you and James stayed with dad the whole journey you didn't want to miss a thing. Me and Liam walked sometimes, but stayed with mum in the B&B's for most of the trip because we kept getting tired. My feet were always hurting when we did stuff like that but you and James always kept going, but now my feet never hurt" I smiled

"yeah what I would give for my comfy hiking boots and a cold bottle of Mountain Dew" we both whispered aloud

"DEEEW!" and gave a small chuckle

"you guys talking about dads hiking trips?" we looked forward and James was standing there with Mia while she held his hands. She looked at us then back at him gave a nod, then walked back up the tunnels to regroup the rest of team "Look Ryan I'm sorry I snapped, you helped us back there and I wasn't sure we were getting Chloe out. I just thought of Mum if she thought one of us wasn't with Lewis the whole time, I just..." I stopped him

"You gave me an order and I didn't follow, I'd be pissed at me too. I'm sorry" We smiled at each other, and then James looked at Lewis

"you doing good little man?" Lewis hugged James's waist

"you don't need to worry about me big bro" James ruffled Lewis's hair and went down on one knee

"perhaps not, but I'm going to anyway".

The rest of the troop assembled in the tunnel behind us. "Steven can you do the honours?" Steven nodded and tapped Simon on the shoulder, the two picked up pace and made their way faster than the rest of us. This decent took us longer than the others, nearly two hours passed before we regrouped with Steven and Simon. Our lips became parched as we continued to ration our supplies, the thought of cold water on our lips began to swim through everyone's mind.

Just as we were about to stop for a breather Steven and Simon returned to the group, Steven gestured down the tunnel

"not far now, not sure how we are going to play this one to be honest" We walked down and entered into a huge cavern filled with the sound of rippling water. It was a beautiful glistening river that reflected silver light off the ceiling and water so pure it could quench the soul even the smell of damp air beckoned us forward. I looked at my water bottle and I wasn't the only one "DON'T GO NEAR THE WATER!" James bellowed and we all looked him "this is the river Styx, touch that and your soul will be claimed by the dead flowing through. Look for a dock and think hard we are going to have to either bribe a ferryman or take his boat"

We made our way through the damp atmosphere and clambered over moist rocks that followed the shore line. They felt damp and water droplets could be heard falling into the water in the distance, but no ripples appeared on the surface. I guessed this was a trick to entice you towards the water and take a sip. We came across a narrow path through the stones and eventually came across a sturdy wooden platform that seemed to protrude into the water and into a mist that had slowly crept over the river. James halted the group drew his sword and walked onto the platform, he crept forward looking for signs of life when he heard "YOU ARE NOT DEAD" the voice echoed all around the cavern and sent a chill up everyone's spine. James quivered slightly but regained command of his actions

"no but we seek passage through" it was quiet for a moment then the voice spoke again

"THEN DIE AND COME BACK" I drew my sword the "shing" of the metal as it left its sheath caused James to turn round and beckon us not to retaliate

"we can give fair payment for safe transport?" the voice did not wait to answer

"you seek to bribe me like so many before you, but I seek no payment. Your kind has become twisted and broken, you are not worthy to board my barge. Lewis shouted across the mist "PLEASE" the water was silent and still as we awaited a reply. Then a great gust of wind blew through and the mist cleared in an instant revealing a 20ft wooden barge. It was not broken and decrepit as we or Hollywood had imagined it would be, but a beautiful black barge with silver ornaments and metal work all around even the ropes were twisted silver strands with the strength to hold bridges. On the front was a dragon made of pure ebony and had glaring silver eyes facing downstream. A cabin rested at the back with steps leading up the left side to the ornate helm. Looking close saw this is where a dark figure stood.

"A pure soul? What business does a pure soul have here?" The figure came into view, again not as expected. He was not a hooded figure or skeleton with bony fingers holding an oar, but a man dressed in familiar attire stood a top looking over the beautifully polished rail on the deck. We stood gasping at the man before us "you're a pathfinder?" said James. The man passed the deck, stopped and looked directly at Lewis

"I was once, but why are you here?" James stood tall

"we seek the ninth gate to save our brother and restore the gates" the man grinned "so that's why I'm back, she has broken them?" James spoke earnestly

"please we have to hurry the fate of our brother and the world is at stake" The man became angry

"THE WORLD, the world is nothing but cut throats, rapists and greed. You see this river" Charon waved his hand out and pointed downstream "it used to be a passage to the depths of the underworld where the unworthy could receive their punishments, but the flow of those failing to pass redemption grew and grew until there were too many. They and the many that came after, have continued fill it so it became the river I sail, the tide never going down. I continue guiding them all in their never ending journey around hell, to their long awaiting punishments. Even those I thought were different who could bring change, the ones I believed could lower the tide and stop the flow have failed. I tried to help them but still the river flowed faster and faster. Humans are so corrupt, why try to save them? You're not the first to come through here trying to save the world, you all end up forgetting that our order weren't supposed to just guide the dead, but guide the living. To help the world become better, but here I am millenniums later and the tide is still no lower if anything the river is more treacherous then ever even for me"

James stood there trying to get his head around everything he said, I stood up and walked forward

"why have you given up?!" I gestured to the group "we haven't, you think we don't know how shitty people are, how much easier it would be just to give up let them all die. We don't look for the easy way out, we march forward and we save the few that are worth saving. We..." the ferryman put his hand up and I paused

"you know nothing, you have all forgotten" and the barge disappeared in a puff of mist. I moved forward stood on the dock and my eyes widening trying to see the barge in the mist and anger filled my lungs

"YOU COWARD!" but we heard nothing back.

It felt like hours, I sat on a rock on the shore line spinning my sword on its point listening to the metal dig into the ground as James walked up and down the length of the dock, thinking and looking for signs of the ferryman's return. I stared at my sword as the symbols and the hogs head I had carved into it flashed before my eyes. I remembered the first time I saw the office, wondering why I was there? Why did we have to help the dead? Why was there all this nonsense in the way in first place? What was the point of it all? I rapped my head for a meaning when I remembered our motto, I stood up and walked onto the dock, took a deep breath and shouted "NE OBLIVISCARIS" I paused waiting to see what would happen but nothing "We do not forget the dead, we protect them, and we are not here to shape the world. We are here so that everyone can remember, that the worthy may seek redemption but the corrupted will atone for their sins" I waited on the dock holding my sword tightly, the mist did not move but a voice could be heard.

"You think the sins seek atonement boy?" I stood firm

"even if they don't, we will make sure they find it".

The boat came back into view pushing up against the dock never making a bow wave

"we will see wont we" The ferry man grinned. A wooden platform came down from the boat and the ferryman gestured us on. We wasted no time and began to board, James came past me put his hand on my shoulder and boarded. No sooner were we on the boat than it shifted from the dock and began its slow trundle down river.

We sat down on the barge, as it made its way down stream and we began losing ourselves in thought as we went further and further into the abyss. I looked up and down the deck, on one side a lantern swung slowly illuminating the walls of the cavern and reflecting an orange glow off the metal work. On the other side was the cabin, solid wood with no windows, a wooden door with silver brackets and two fixed lanterns lit either side. Upon the door engraved into the woodwork I recognised the rough cut dug out etchings of the Star of David, it looked chiselled as thought something had been dug out of it.

We didn't talk much to each other for fear the ferryman would change his mind and we would finally see if the river had a bottom or not. We just watched as the river passed us by never splashing, but made the trickling sound all the same. I know the souls made the river and I swear I could see faces in the water or the light was just tricking me into seeing them, but there was something beautiful about it. It was like flowing silk or mercury with no froth or bubble just the smooth creamy texture of liquid going in one direction. I looked back at the ferryman whose eyes where fixated on the route ahead and caught the eye of Chloe who was spinning her Rune Gauntlet sending messages to my dad and Brian.

"Charon" I looked puzzled at her "his name is Charon as in Kiron" she looked up at me, smiled and looked back down at her gauntlet continuing to spin it methodically

"thanks" I said. I stood up and walked up to the helm where Charon stood his body swaying with the motion of the boat. I fixated on him before opening my mouth not sure what I wanted to know first "Why are you are still here? How are you not? You know, dead?" he looks at me and I see his face fully for the first time, an older man with a short white beard, tipped with tinges of black. The scars on his face from battles past making him look more grizzled "what makes you think I'm alive?" he paused looking for me to flinch but I stood my ground and he looked back down river "We die too you know, we can seek redemption or fade away from existence in purgatory" he looked at me again "or we can descend into hell and keep making life difficult for the dammed demons of this plain" This put a smile on his face as it looked like he was recalling memories of his youth "When this river formed, we would take little boats down with us to reach these gates, many perished in the waters as the dead pulled them in whenever they could. So we made this and other large boats to sail the waters safely, when my crew were killed protecting this stupid king that had killed thousands to build his monuments. I had two options, go to my gate, or stay on the boat. I chose to stay on my boat, before long when I thought about leaving, I couldn't. I was now part of the boat guiding all to their destinations, I considered it an honour at the time. But then people began to forget about this place and its purpose, until it faded from everyone's memory, and then faded all together into stories and legend. It was then I began to see people for who they really are" I looked at him as he told his story

"are there more like you?" I kept staring at him watching his expressionless face

"no, I'm the only one left" It was stupid but I had to ask even at the risk of him changing his mind

"why did you decided to help us?" as the words left my mouth I felt stupid expecting him to stop and throw us over board

"you are doing the duty I set out to do when I was your age, everyone here trusts you with their life, young Master Campbell" he paused and looked down at the helm "but I'm not helping you, beyond the river, once you depart you will see why we have hell. I'm just letting you go see the souls of the world in their purest form of corruption and greed. So you and the rest of the world can see and remember that mankind never learned, and deserves it fate" I looked at the figure in front of me stricken with hatred for humans and made my way back down to the main deck. He helps us but isn't helping us? He doesn't believe in the quest? How does he know my name?

"Well he sounded fucking cheery" Simon said as he looked up at the figure on the helm in the distance. I looked back as I went down the last step

"yeah, guess too much time down here you see nothing but the worst of people. Still, he let us on board and I'm not going to question that anymore." I thought to myself, he can't have completely given up on people. Even if in his mind, we are just heading towards corruption and death there has to be something there.

I took my seat again beside Chloe and asked if she had had any reply from the surface, she looked troubled

"no and we should have heard something by now, those creatures will be on the surface already what if..." I stopped her "you've seen Brian shoot, Grandad is with him and my dad is with them leading the defences. Even if there was no other finders in the fort they wouldn't lose, frankly the odds seems a little unfair" I tried to sound jovial, I looked her in the eye and winked, and she smiled and stared down stream.

James was standing at the bow of the ship admiring the wood and metal work of the dragon that adorned the front. Mia walked up to him and put her arm on his shoulder to get his attention and they both look forward at the dimly lit bleak of the path ahead, Mia speaks softly to James

"how far do you think we've travelled? Feels like miles but every bit of this place looks the same" James continued to stare forward

"not quite" His brow narrowed as he tried to focus "the boat is getting faster" He continued to look and then the reason we were speeding up became apparent "we're about to hit rapids" he turned to us all "everyone get up, find rope and tie yourself to something" we all scrambled for our packs to get rope and tied ourselves to whatever part of the boat we were closest too. As we did the rush of wind picked up and we could feel the boat lifting and heaving over the now rushing and thrashing water, the lamp began to sway to and fro furiously its light dancing from barge to wall. I looked at Charon who's gaze was not breaking from the road ahead he didn't sway with the boat as it rocked he remained steadfast, unyielding to the fury of the waters. I can feel the boat lift from left to right as we begin to shoot through tunnels up and down, the boat pitching harder left and right. My body felt like it was being thrown around on the Waltzers fairground ride. I could see everyone holding onto the side of the boat for dear life griping tight, some closing their eyes and their legs flailing trying to find a grip. My arm held the wooden beam and I tried to hold my pack close. Lewis was close to Simon who had him gripped tightly, I looked over trying to see that everyone was ok.

Just as my head lifted I could see James scrambling to grip Mia as her rope snapped, she tried to grab what she could but began rolling and hurtling towards the back of the boat banging her head on the deck. I let go of my pack letting if fly off into the black either, I leapt from my perch and wrapped my arms around her waist as she came to me. My rope pulled tight around my waist and flung against the wooden edging with a thud. Mia flopped in my arms unconscious as I took grip of the wooden rail once again watching as the water continued to wash around us. I closed my eyes trying to block the pain of the rope on my waist, the bruising on my back or the tension on my arms. The black engulfed my vision; memories of the old boat in Willy Wonka came flashing before my eyes as I crushed them shut trying not to think about the motion. Just as I felt my grip starting to fail me, I could feel the boat begin to slow, the rush of wind dying down and becoming a low rustle in my ears. As the tunnel opened once again into a cavern the fury of the water became still again allowing everyone to regain their footing and loosen their grip. James cut his cord and rushed over as I lay Mia down softly on the deck her red hair now untied draped down her shoulders. I looked at Simon who was loosening himself and Lewis who looked unscathed by the ride. One of our companions not so unscathed found an empty barrel that was tied down and released his last meal. I looked at the dock slowly drifting towards us and turned to Charon to scathe him for his lack of warning about the rapids, only to see he wasn't there. We searched the boat as James and Chloe got Mia back on her feet a little dazed and holding her head, He was gone with no sign or trace, below deck one of our group found a small collection of supplies, and there was my pack sitting next to them. I inspected it with curiosity as I last saw it disappear into nowhere, but here it was dry and undamaged. I looked at the others then shouldered my pack as we all began to disembark and head down the next tunnel, no-one felt like stopping to eat as we all struggled to find our land legs trying not to sway on the level ground. Mia still holding her head walked up to me

"thank you" she said softly and walked further into shore. I Looked back just in time for the mist to engulf the boat once more and disappear from sight.

# Chapter 18

## The Rot
### (The Fort)

"How are you doing lad? Trigger finger getting numb yet?" Grandad shouted as he loaded his next magazine

"I thought this was just the warm up round Popp's don't tell me I need to get the blanket out for your afternoon nap" Brian laughed he was always more confident when he was in the zone, years of online gaming and listening to him on the headset had shown me that. Grandad retorted

"they be fighting words pup! I'll have you tucked in your bed looking for a bedtime story before my arm gets tired" he slams the magazine then goes to take aim, just as he goes to focus on his next target he spots a great sand storm brewing in the distance racing forward like a tidal wave moving swiftly to crash against the shore "shit! MAJOR! ROT INBOUND SOUTH EAST 1 MILE!!" Grandad then spun around and began scrambling around his pack unsure if the Dad had heard him he shouted again "ROT IMBOUND". Brian turned to him with puzzled and troubled look

"what is a rot?" Grandad found black cloths covered in silver symbols in his bag pushed his rifle next to the 50 cal and tried to cover both with it, Grandad shouts once more urgently "MAJOR WE'VE GOT A ROT!!" this time he caught dads attention and was pointing forward frantically towards the storm now visible to all. Dad started shouting to all units scrambling captains and lieutenants to cloth everything they could

"what is it?" Brian asked earnestly going to grab a cloth to cover his rifle, Grandad panted before answering "here get your gun under this and all the ammo you can, honestly lad we're not sure no-one has seen it in over a thousand years, but what we know is anything unprotected will decay and flake away in seconds including us, so wrap your cloak tight around you and cover you rifle as best you can. Whatever you do, do not breathe in the sand, use your cloak over your face" Grandad scrambled to cover more gear. In the distance the folly had disappeared in the storm which was now only a few hundred yards out as Brian and everyone took cover trying to shield themselves and their weapons. The wind swept around and engulfed the fortress, red dust kicked up blocking all vision as everyone scrambled trying not to breathe in the sand. Brian could barely see through the thin slits of his cloak as some who hadn't moved in time fell to the ground gasping and reaching out, he went to get up to help them only to be pinned down by Popp's who began to shout through his cloak

"don't be foolish, the moment you try to help your dead too, just keep in cover and wait till it blows over" Brian muffled by the cloak tried to shout back

"but what about the demons?" Grandad answered

"They can't be out in this either probably took cover to wait it out" the wind began to sweep faster and louder. Brian could see the metal boxes they didn't get covered in time, he watched as the back-up ammo they needed began to turn orange, flake then disintegrate before his eyes, followed by all the ammo it held

"why doesn't the rock were sitting on disintegrate?" Brian shouted

"Because it's from here and it's not an alloy, remember anything we bring in that isn't protected by runes, is fucked" They kept their backs to the wall and huddled up waiting for the storm to pass. Brian's thoughts drifted to Chloe and his friends, where were they? Were they still ok? Would he see them again?

Commander Mcmail sat in her office holding her hands together, locked hand in hand on the desk. Her eyes piercing, staring at the two sitting in front of her looking for the answers she already knew but wanting her fears confirmed "exactly how many went down?" her voice quivered with anger but at the same time calm, as she accepted there was nothing she could do to change the answer. Before she could begin a scalding the two in front of her the door burst open with a soldier standing in the doorway "Commander your needed in the control room immediately" She leapt from her desk

"you two don't move" Jason and Dixon looked at each other not muttering a word as the Commander stormed out. The command station was frantic with communications coming in as officers tried to issue orders "what's going on?" Colonel Hendricks looked up from a scribe he was dictating too

"It's not good, if these reports are anything to go by, it's a rot" the Commander gripped the railing tight

"what's the status of our defences" the Colonel kept his composure

"they didn't have much warning and reports are brief as many are trying to maintain cover, only the veterans still carry cloths to deal with this so we expect our heavy weapons to suffer badly" "how badly" The colonel looks at his sheet trying to look as though it was a minor detail "we expect heavy weapons to be down 86% standard down 35% and casualties" Hendricks paused for a moment "casualties 40%" he looks up at the Commander dead in the eye "once the storm clears and everything starts back up again, we will know" She bows her head holding the railing

"may hell and or heaven have mercy on us, and the souls we protect, give us strength".

# Chapter 19

## Level 6
### Burning Tombs

The group having regained their land legs were making quick progress through the passages to the sixth level. We didn't stop long for refreshment only to check that the supplies found on the barge weren't poisonous using one of Chloe's runes spells. Not wanting to break the pace and walking in silence with his own thoughts, James neglected to send scouts up ahead and was shocked when he could feel the aura pulsing from the cavern ahead. He froze only for a moment before continuing forwards and entering the next clearing. He slowly walked into the largest chamber yet, what could be described as nothing less than a huge volcanic crater lay before him. Searing molten magma pulsed in the lake below like scalding blisters bursting across the surface "and here I was worried I wasn't going to get a chance to work on my tan on this trip" Simon chuckled as he peered round the group looking up at the large convex ceiling and taking in the large expanse of the room. The heat was nothing to be unexpected they were in hell after all and some runes on their armour dealt very specifically with the intense heats possible, that being said this was pushing it and their brows began to perspire just looking in. As they looked closer the whole cavern was lined with arches blocked with huge rocks, some had crumbled and magma waterfalls were flowing down into the lake
"Over there to the left" shouted Chloe, a winding path going back and forth amongst the tombs was visible going in different directions, up and down from the towering heights of the cavern like a huge football stadium and even some that crept

inside the crater towards the lake. The same sort of route could be seen on the right, but the paths in that direction had already crumbled and looked impassable.

We were about to start forward when James halted us again "look at the arches" we scrutinised the arches carefully and noticed different symbols on the peak stone of each "anyone got any ideas?" Chloe began spinning her gauntlet for inspiration as if one of the runes would tell her what to look for. Everyone else just kept looking around the room for ideas

"that one!" we looked round to our smallest companion and I spoke

"why do you think it's that one Lewis?" Lewis looked shyly at everyone looking at him

"I saw it on the big clock in the office and I liked it" he was pointing towards a symbol that looked a lot like a ships helm, I tried not to sound condescending

"if that symbol was for anything surely it would have been for the last level little man" Chloe spoke up from behind me

"he might be right" I looked at her awaiting the explanation "the wheel is one of the least explained or understood symbols on the plate but does fall in line with the sixth trial if the symbols go in order

"and what if they don't?" James interjected; Chloe shrugged her shoulders

"it's the best we've got at the moment". Unsure how to test the water James decided the only thing to do was to go ahead and walk in front of the arch with the helm symbol above, he walked past slowly so as to fully test its challenge. Nothing happened, no breaking of the stone, no lava waterslide just nothing, he let out a sigh of relief and wiped the sweat from his brow. James nodded to the rest of us who began to follow in single file up the track, we began the winding ascent which was far from straight forward, it began taking us round to the right side of the chamber across narrow paths that barely held together often forcing us to grip the wall beside us just to get past. My foot almost slipped at one point and I watched as the rocks fell below knocking and triggering one of the tomb walls to crack and flow yet another molten stream. As we approached to the top of the cavern the heat forced a wind to wisp around the top, which made walking even more difficult. I could see James trying to peer round at each archway looking for the symbol changing direction occasionally, as we moved further round, the symbols seemed more faint and the path more narrow, which forced James to have Simon and Steven hold him as he hung out just to see them. Breathing was laboured as the pulsing of the heat made everyone except Lewis feel woozy. Beginning to descend in the direction we wanted our minds wandered to the thumping of our feet and the moisture touching our skin. I held Lewis close to the wall over a narrow step watching dirt crumble with each movement, We crept onwards and just as we approached a level point of thicker ledge, I looked behind us at those following and spotted at the rear of our group private Henderson, he was dreary eyed and swaying. I started shouting "Will, WILL!" he missed his step, I lunged past the others diving to the edge and grabbing the ledge, reaching out just missing his hand as he slid down the slope grabbing hold of the arch two levels below. He stared me in the eyes looking at me as we felt the rumble and heard the stone crack, I saw the fear in his eyes as the others tried to throw a rope down to him. It was too late, the rock blew out with the force of the magma behind it and I watched as he was flung into the crater. I was pulled up but continued staring into the lake where I watched him disappear, If only I was faster if I had kept a closer look. I knew James felt the same way but remained stoic trying to get my attention

"You tried, if you couldn't catch him, I don't think anyone could" James stood up pulling me up with him "we have to keep moving before the rest crumbles" he stood tall and shouted to the group "if you're not feeling right tell someone and everyone keep an eye on each other" I stood up and re-joined Lewis along the trail still looking where I saw Will disappear

"I'm sorry big bro if I wasn't here you could have got to him" I looked round at Lewis forcing a smile

"If you weren't here I would never forgive myself for not getting him, your my first charge" I put my arm on his shoulder to reassure him and tried not to look back.

We moved onwards along the path which did not prove as treacherous, that was until we lost the symbol. James raced going back and forth between all the arches around us we couldn't spot the wheel

"what the hell!" James slammed his fists against the wall in anger and I heard rubble drop in the distance "seriously can we not catch a break" just as he looked up at the stone facing him he could see veins of silver in the cracks, he beckoned me "Ryan come here, you see that" I peered in looking at it

"magnesium? But why hasn't it ignited already?" James looked closer at the silver veins "maybe it's not close enough or hot enough, but look it goes into all the arches towards the exit. If it's like the ones in the caves with dad it should shoot along and hopefully trigger all the remaining doors, we can then sneak by and get out of here" Chloe was the first to interject

"and what if it works, we could have lava both above and below us flowing not to mention if there is any deposits that could explode at any moment" I looked at her

"your welcome to keep looking for the symbols but I can't see any" James had his fingers in the crack

"it's a risk, but nothing else has been anything less so far. Let's see what happens, everyone get ready to run Simon take Ryan's bag, Ryan carry Lewis" I nodded and got ready hoisting Lewis onto my back. James took Mia's spear and lowered its tip into an already damaged tomb below that had a small stream of magma trickling out of it, as he got back to his feet holding the orange glow at length he dug it into the crack waiting. Sure enough sparks started but nothing happened, we waited watching it, all of a sudden out of the vein it began spluttering and shooting out of the crack along different trails activating the traps, tomb after tomb cracked and flowed more lava to the crater leaving a clear and fairly accessible path. I smiled at James who looked back me with triumph before widening his eyes and then focusing, he watched as one thread began to rush back to the entrance of the cavern. I looked over just as it fizzled out in a puff of smoke, a great sign of relief could be heard all round.

"Right then let's get a move on" said Simon, as we took two steps forward without warning we could hear the fizz again and BOOM went the entrance, the earth began to shake and tremble, without a second thought James shouted

"GET A MOVE ON!!" We sprinted down the path running like a stampede fleeing a predator, I glimpsed behind only for a moment to see the walls cascading down, mounds of dirt, rubble and lava rippling down the walls racing towards us "GET A MOVE ON, COME ON! COME ON!" James shouted again Simon who was weighed down by two packs, was still flying with speed

"you don't have to tell me twice!" the lake below began to rock and spurt causing hot puddles to be thrown onto the path ahead "ouch, shit  WATCH YOUR STEP!" as a corner of Mia's cloak got splashed, melted and fluttered away. Running as fast as I could I heard shouting behind me, someone had tripped and I saw two more figures falling into the crater. We got to the exit and dived into the arch rolling down the steep slope as a cloud of dust blew in behind us blocking out all light and the rocks that fell blocked the way back crashing down the archway. Tumbling forward everyone landed in a great heap with little light

"whoever has their hand on my tit remove it or lose digits" Mia groaned from under the pile "it's my hand girl, do you even have any padding?" Chloe tried to wriggle free of the pile "Simon that had better be your dagger!" Steven shouted again, Simon laughed

"easy, cave-ins don't quite do it for me"

We regained our feet and lit some lamps looking at the now blocked passage behind us, Simon threw a pebble at the pile "don't suppose we really want to be going back that way anyway. I hope there's an escalator or something at the other end heading back up, this walk is never ending" James began to look a little beat down "who did we lose?" Only he seemed to register that our party was smaller again

"Herron and Phelps" I answered, James seemed beaten down at this news, so I took charge "let's get some rest, even some sleep if you can manage it but mind and don't use up your rations" James nodded at the order and we set up in a circle using a few oil lamps in the centre for light, even with Lewis's soul our armour seemed dimly lit. Simon and Steven fell asleep instantly using his packs for a pillow, a few of the others tried to do the same. Lewis and I lay down but both of us were wide awake so just reminisced about days passed. Chloe sat with her gauntlet pressed against her but instead of sending messages she just sat quietly, I leaned over

"I'm sure they're all fine, probably even busier than us" My words didn't seem to comfort her but she curled over anyway maybe to actually sleep, but most likely pretending so no-one asked how she was. James sat with Mia's head on his shoulder, she spoke softly to him as he bowed his head

"I'm ok, try and get some sleep, we still have three levels to go and I don't think they are going to get easier" Mia nodded looked at me then curled up next to Chloe.

After an hour almost everyone was asleep, everyone except James who was still staring at the lamp and me looking at the now blocked entrance. He got up and strode down the tunnel passage a bit, I got up and went after him put my hand on his shoulder

"You ok?" he turned around to look at me, his eye were blood shot and filled with sadness "I'm not doing well am I?" I tilted my head confused

"What do you mean?" James shook his head "I've lost several people under my charge already and the mission isn't even over, what kind of leader am I. I didn't even notice Henderson I should have been looking, I..." I stopped him

"James, hell doesn't normally look like this, no-one could have been prepared for this and most importantly If we didn't follow you, none of us could have made it this far. You know all of our best skills and traits and you are always willing to take the first step." He looked at me

"and what about you, you happy babysitting? don't you want to lead the group?" Memories of my dark jealous feelings crept upon me, I felt guilty for my actions but looking into my brothers eyes I steeled my resolve and I put my other hand on his other shoulder

"I will follow you brother, not because of your rank, but because I believe Lewis's best chance lies with you and no-one else" James straightens resting his hand on the hilt of his sword

"keep me on point will you" I grip his shoulders tight

"till the end" He embraces me and we return to the group where Simon and Steven are sitting up sharing some biscuits. I scoff to lighten the mood

"tucking into a hob nob again are you Simon" He sits stuffing his face with the biscuit

"shhh shhuuu ut uup dick" He blustered biscuit and I grinned. James sat down

"you two able to keep watch while we take a kip?" they nodded and James and I curled over, the fatigue of everything that had happened hit me hard and I fell asleep almost instantly, never had a slumber hit so hard as that moment.

# Chapter 20

## The Storm passes The Fight resumes
### (The Fort)

Brian was sat still huddled up in the nest waiting for the storm to pass, Popp had gotten up to find something in another nest during the storm keeping his cloak wrapped tightly around him. Brian was sat thinking about everyone wandering in hell below. He thought about what Popp's had said, about what he would say to Chloe when he saw her. He thought about what he should be saying right now, he never even considered the rune gauntlet he was given, but there again it never left his pack. He carefully tried to open his pack to find it, it didn't take much effort. It was spinning around like crazy different symbols lighting up in sequences

"best check my messages then, she's gonna kill me" he began messaging back about the assault on the fort being careful not to let his cloak slip, he messaged about how he and Popps were doing fine, but currently hiding in a massive sand storm. He wasn't sure how to word it in a way that she wouldn't be worried about him but knew that's facts were always her preferred news, good or bad.

Just as he finished his message and looked at the gauntlet expectantly the atmosphere all around him changed. In that moment the wind died down with no warning, the dust settled all around and Brian could see the fortress coming into view all around him. Everyone was coming to their feet looking at what remained; everything else was also coming to its feet, Major Williams bellowed almost instantly "battle stations!!" Brian flung the cloth from his rifle but spun around looking for Popp's

"Popp's, POPP'S!" he spotted a cloak and armour on the ground near his nest and his heart sunk. He gazed at the cloth looking for a stir or a sign of life, but nothing happened

"get your head in the game boy!" Brian spun round to see Popp's jumping up the stairs with the few sniper magazines he could find left intact in the fortress "come on the game isn't up yet" Brian grinned back at him trying not give away his relief "still think you can beat me old man?" Grandad shouldered his rifle "still know I can kick your arse lad" He took aim immediately and let loose the first round, then patted his rifle

"that's my girl, make me proud" the figures in the distance where all shaking off the sand and began to shout, screech and wail with excitement of being able to charge once again. Brian's trigger finger was well rested and he looked at his emerging targets, in that moment he looked up and could see a smaller dark cloud, He shouted hoping anyone would hear him

"FURYS!" All snipers raised their rifles at the incoming flurry of large bat like creatures now descending on them. Some swooped down trying to pick soldiers up and carry them off; Brian swapped to his assault rifle set it to single fire then began popping them as quick as he could. Grandad used his side arm then grabbed sword in hand spotted one that took notice of Brian and was about to grab him, just as Brian swapped out his magazine the fury's claws went to grab him from behind, but Popps lunged at it burying his sword in it chest and he watched as it dropped to the ground off the tower wailing then going silent

"ugly little bastards" he patted Brian on the shoulder and they shot what remained of the screeching vermin. The creatures of hell didn't seem diminished at all by the sand storm and were determined more than ever to take the fort.

In the office the scribes sprung to life once again one scribe read aloud

"The rot has lifted, few casualties" a small cheer of relief could be heard amongst the staff, few casualties was better news than they had hoped for. "Fury incursion repelled, enemy forces still strong, defensive operations resumed" The Commander still clutching the railing eased her grip and stood tall.

"Have the Citadel contacted us yet?"

"No sir, no word yet and we've had no further reports from other sites" she nods, not the words she wanted to hear but sometimes no news was good news. She nodded to the Colonel then went out of the Command station and into the main lobby; defensive positions had been set up outside the entrance to hell and soldiers where all on alert. She then looked up at the Great seal on the wall staring at the ninth symbol. She whispered to herself

"I hope you lot are having an easier time of it down there". A look of sadness came across her face as she wished she had put a more experienced crew together to test the ninth gate, she was now powerless to do anything about it. Taking one more glance at the wilted light she headed toward the auditorium, where Clerics were attempting to gather and calm the present and arriving souls "how are things here?" she asked one of the clerical staff "honestly not good ma'am we have had near 50 souls fade before their due time they were all supposed to be going down tomorrow. We've tried to re assure the others but the time frame is depleting fast, our only bit of luck is that the arrivals gate is slow today" The Commander nods

"do what you can, this ordeal isn't over yet" she straightens up "make sure they are in their groups I want them ready to go the moment the gates are back up"

"yes sir" the Commander smiles at the other Clerics then walks away from the auditorium back to the Commander Centre. Worried more now than ever for the souls awaiting redemption and the souls that may be joining. She then continues to check on operations and other personnel to keep both theirs and her mind at ease.

# Chapter 21

## Level 7
### Labyrinth

"HE'S OK!" I woke up startled to Chloe jumping up with excitement "Brian, Popp's, your Dad the fortress they're ok they are in some kind of sandstorm it could be a typo, the man can't spell to save his life but he's ok" tears well up in her eyes at the news and a sense of relief swelled in me, hearing that they were ok justified our risk and resolve at least in that moment. James stood up

"then our mission is far from lost and they are depending on us to see it through, whether they know it or not". Everyone felt rested spurred on to see it through, we re-assembled our packs dropping any dead weight and checked our weapons.

"oh man that feels so much better" my shoulder having felt the pressure of carrying my pack (even though sometimes giving it to Simon) and welcomed the lighter weight. We began making our way down the passage with our spirits raised almost as high as when we entered hell to begin with, our knew found strength had us setting a quick pace as we made our way below.

It wasn't long before our familiar tunnel began to open out once more, into another large expansive cavern. But this time we weren't able to see our trial laid before us, this time a huge 15ft wall stood ahead. Looking up and down we saw one entrance to the 200 yard expansive wall and had no idea just how far it went back. "Ryan think you can give me a boost" I looked at Simon who passed and walked in front of me and I looked at him confused "I might be able to get up to the top of the wall and get a birds eye view, it doesn't take genius to figure out a maze when you see one, so a birds eye view couldn't hurt" I looked at James who nodded and I backed up against the wall

"Ready" I said and I stood with my hands locked waiting to vault Simon up. He ran at me with all his speed put his right foot into my hands and with our combined momentum he just managed to grab the top of the 15ft wall and hoist himself up. He stood on the ledge pacing back and forth trying to get a view of the path ahead. I looked over to Steven "can you give me a hand, this buggers gonna be heavy when he comes back down" Steven and two others came over and we locked arms ready for Simon to jump down

"drop me and I will beat your ass's" Simon lowered himself as much as he could then leapt backwards into our arms "ooo la la boys I could get use to this" he laughed and we let go letting him scramble to his feet. James walked forward "what did you see?" Simon brushed the dirt off his armour

"sure enough it's a maze that is plain, only what I didn't see was the exit and because of the height I could barely make out the path. From what I did see though hugging routes to the right and trying to find the middle will be our best option" James nodded his thanks then turned to the group

"gear up eyes sharp, this could be a simple maze, it could be Pan's Labyrinth from legend. If that's the case then there will be trials inside as well as monsters, worst of all, a huge Minotaur that will gorge you and think nothing of it. Stay close swords out" Simon walked up to Lewis, he took out one of his reserve knifes out spun it around his hand and fingers playfully before putting it in its sheath and offering the hilt to Lewis

"just in case little man" Lewis's eye lit up and he looked at me for approval I said

"go ahead you with a knife might be the least of my worries today" and he grabbed the knife looking at it with awe before I spoke "remember it is not a toy, Simon has been practising that stuff for years. Keep it close and in its sheath, pray you don't have to use it"

We began walking into the maze, the walls were stone bricks

lined with algae and tree roots running over the ground. Running water trickling over rocks could be heard faintly in the background and floral smells filled the air. Every so often Simon would go up and get a view of the route to proceed forward, it was a slow trek but soon enough we were deep into the maze. We walked so many twists and turns, sometimes having to double back on ourselves for five minutes to get a route forward. It felt like two hours before we eventually we reached what we guessed was the centre of the maze. A beautiful marble fountain in the shape of balance scales, with the purest spring water sat dead centre surrounded by a garden of flowers, vines and intricate stone work to rival any botanical garden. I was stood looking in awe when I heard

"STOP" one of the privates had put his hand in the fountain and just as James yelled and he drank the water. The private froze still, his eyes horror stricken awaiting his fate. Every second felt like a minute in dead silence, but nothing happened, James approached him slowly and spoke softly "Michael how do you feel? can you move all of your limbs" Michael moved his fingers, arms, legs and patted down his body

"I feel fine" it was a further few seconds but it felt like a further 10 minutes. But nothing happened, it was a plain water fountain nothing more. The group began to refill their flasks and rest a minute. Simon sat on a stone perch looking at the world around gazing at the flowers that bloomed

"not a bad wee spot, almost forget we're sitting in hell to be honest" he watches a small stream flowing through some of the cracks in the wall and start chuckling to himself, I look bemused and ask him what he is laughing at "how does the rock pee?" he pauses for effect "he Dwaynes his Johnson!" Most of us sighed, but Lewis started laughing and I looked about to ask if he even got the joke, but to be honest I didn't want him to stop laughing. That little moment of laughter was all the joy I needed right now and I didn't want it to end, but it was always going too "gear up, it's time to move on" James felt too idle in this little Oasis and we got to our feet, we began again down our path and the trickling sound of water began fading away once more.

We were walking along our path exiting the oasis trying to remain wary, but the calm of the spring was all over us like a warm blanket from snow. I began to feel safe, before I looked back just in time to see the Scales tip and what was once the lower was now the upper scale, we started to hear the familiar crack and rumble of rocks breaking, I hold Lewis close as we all braced to see what would happen. Without warning the stone walls and floor all began shifting and moving like and airport travellators, everyone was falling over being thrown in different directions away from each other. I held Lewis close swearing I wouldn't lose him, I watched as everyone disappeared behind rock walls. We were rolling and bumping avoiding the walls as they closed on each other when the motion stopped and we lay there checking it was over, I tried to get to my legs quickly to survey the area. Helping Lewis to his feet I looked left and right down the passage

"IS EVERYONE OK?" I heard James shout and everyone answered

"Steven and Sarah ok"

"Mia and Michael ok" I heard them all and relaxed a little

"Ryan and Lewis ok" looking at Lewis and I smiled

"Simon think you can see everyone?" James shouted. We thought the fun was over but right then, rock crumbled again and I grabbed Lewis expecting the floor to shuffle once more. But the floor and walls didn't move. I looked up just in time to see the roof come down and shut flush on the walls of the maze, blocking out all external light and sound. My armour dimly lit with the light of Lewis, I sparked my lamp looking left and right down a now dark tunnel "everyone ok?" I called out but no-one answered, I then shouted "CAN ANYONE HEAR ME!?" still silence, everyone was now cut off from one another I looked down "you ok little man?" Lewis looks at me and nods, looking up I say "so which way do you want left" I shine my lamp down the passage "or right" Lewis ponders this and just points to which I start moving "right it is then" We begin walking down the trail, following its twists and turns always shouting to find someone but no-one answered "it's been an hour, surely we should have seen someone by now" I looked at Lewis "don't suppose you're carrying a map are you?" Lewis shook his head grinning, silence held the tunnel close and I listened. As we walked cautiously minding our step a horrible angry sound erupted all around the chamber shaking the walls, with the echo I couldn't tell what direction it was coming from

"was that a cow?" There was a slight pause "Ryan?" Lewis looked at me puzzled. I lifted my lamp shining it down the passage we had just come from, emerging from the darkness a creature at least 8ft tall of solid muscle and fur with arrows sticking out its shoulders. Horns as white as chalk and the huge face of a bull, it stood looking at me

"Lewis, get ready to run"

"why it might be friendly" I tried to move Lewis slowly behind me backing up cautiously keeping the beast in my sights

"because that's blood dripping off It's hoof Lewis" It lets out another roar, grunts and begins to charge "LEWIS LETS GO" I grab Lewis pick him up and start running, choosing as many turns as possible so the creature can't keep momentum. I can hear him crashing into the tight turns roaring with anger, Lewis spots it behind us "he's catching up Ryan" these words echo in my head, I can't outrun it even with every twist and turn it gains ground. It spots me at one junction and rushes forward head down, I manage to narrowly dodge its charge, the concussion hitting the wall disorienting it only for a moment and rubble splashes on my back as I sprint away. As I run round the next corners I eventually see the next passage is a long straight, knowing the Minotaur will catch us on this next turn I run half way down, put down Lewis and tell him to run. Unsheathing my sword I turn back and look down where we came "don't stop whatever you hear Lewis just keep running" The Minotaur emerges from the corner and grunts once again looking right at me. Tilting its huge head it kicks the ground, snorts and begins charging towards me, I crouch bracing and awaiting its impact in the hope I can land a blow deadly enough to save Lewis. My armour now glowing brightly and arcing with white light, brighter and more intense as the creature gets closer. 30ft from me and it lowers its head further to avoid the light, it is ready to impale me but I don't flinch. Just then I see in slow motion whistling past my ear a silver dagger hurtle towards the creature landing deep in its thigh, the creature stumbles and begins to drop. I lift myself, run forward and leap against the wall for height. The horns rush underneath me and I come down burying my glowing sword into its back and watch the light flow into the creature. The dull roar echoes everywhere, a haunting noise reverberated all around, I twist my sword and the creature is silenced, its muscles going limp and casting dust. Remembering the dagger I dig it out the thigh and I shout "Simon? You there? Couldn't have timed that better if you tried mate" as I walked down the passage wiping my sword and the dagger I look and see just Lewis standing there "where's Simon?" Lewis looks at me with a slight grin

"he's not here" I look at the small blade balancing in my hand

"so this, was you?" he nods grinning widely " you best have it back then, nice shot and, thanks" I smile and hug him

"what was that light Ryan?" I thought about it myself, I had almost forgot it happened "grandad says it happens when we fight for those we care about. It made me feel stronger, faster and braver" satisfied with the answer Lewis draws my attention

"look I found something" he stood pointing at a corner of rock, faintly drawn on the wall was a sketch of scales like the water fountain, he spotted more and we followed them until we could see a flickering light up ahead. I edged quietly so as not to make any sound and peer around the corner. I see familiar faces and look down

"it's ok Lewis, its them" we walk round to be greeted by my brother and the rest

"are we all here?" I ask as I look round taking a head count

"wait where's Sarah?" Steven answered but he sounded as though he had been choked and his eyes were red with sorrow

"she didn't make it, she was with me when that thing found us" I looked at him

"the arrows, those were yours?" Steven stared at his bow

"It snuck up behind us, she tried to attack it, but it impaled and trampled her. I shot it with my arrows and gave chase but it fled, I tried to save… but I couldn't…" Mia spoke up "it's not your fault Steven you couldn't save her, no-one could have" He looked down the passage un-sheathing his sword

"it's still in there" I put my hand up

"Not anymore" I tried to sound re-assuring "Lewis crippled its leg and I stuck my sword through it, it's going nowhere" Steven walked towards me stopped then put his hand out to shake

"thank you" I grabbed his whole arm and looked at James who nodded with approval, I looked at the others

"did anything attack you guys?" "We got a couple of ghouls and harpies" said James

"and we had a fawn kept playing pipes to distract us but nothing we couldn't handle" said Mia. The next passage lay before us and we all felt compelled to leave the labyrinth behind as quick as we could, wasting no more time we proceeded forward. Only one more trial before the ninth gate

"Hurrrrry now my pet, not long"

# Chapter 22

## The Assault Part 1
### (The Fort)

Up until now taking down the demons and other creatures had been an almost playful routine, Pathfinders were after all a large group of soldiers who spent their entire lives defending themselves at close quarters and saw little threat to their defences from targets running at a distance. But the forces of hell were merely getting their weapons into place as everyone would come to realise. As the enemy front line continued to be held back, a sense of over confidence had filled the Fortress. Just as Major Williams was joking with one of the Captains huge fire balls began being hurtled into the sky towards the fortress, like missiles they came crashing in and around the stone keep. Soldiers were trying to maintain cover while trying to keep their quarry suppressed. Major Campbell could be heard over the ensuing barrage

"WE ARE LOW ON AMMO BE READY TO DEFEND THE GATE, SWORDS MAKE SURE YOU HAVE A SWORD" Brian and Popps aimed at as many of the larger targets as possible, another huge roar erupted shaking and echoing across the plain. A huge stone hand rose out of the crater and another massive creature this time a stone giant sprung from the hole. As it crawled out and began crashing forward, it started digging its great hand into the soil and hurtling boulders at the fortress. Several nests and towers were crushed into oblivion and the boulders disintegrated causing soldiers to scatter all around. Major Williams shouted into the square "FIRE EVERYTHING WE HAVE LEFT!!" from all directions mortars and rockets flew whistling through the air, a massive barrage of ordinance that began to rain on the giant and its surroundings. What could only described as one of the most impressive displays of incendiary mayhem ensued reducing the creature to pebbles. The fortress once again erupted with cheers, but the enemy's front line had not diminished and not stopped advancing.

That was it, all the heavy artillery had been spent and the enemy knew it. That was all we had left and now, they are coming.

# Chapter 23

## Level 8
### The Tournament

Working our way down the passage we start hearing a dull noise that rises and falls every 10 minutes, it is like a chant then foot stomping and then silence. Not being deterred we continued forward working our way down the narrow passages and eventually entered the next chamber towards a black nothing. Lit only by our torches and what little light would shine on our armour we start crossing what looked like a large stone bridge onto a huge centre platform. The bridge was harmless enough and once on the platform walking forward we felt safer but our vision did not improve, looking around we can't see anything not even the edge of the platform. We hold our weapons up awaiting an attack from creatures or something to come rushing at us, but nothing came. As we reach what I guessed was the centre of the room, the floor drops a few inches down knocking us all off our feet. Looking back the bridge we crossed was crumbling away now gone into the pit below. Getting to our feet we look around readying our weapons our nerves on edge, James called out "in a circle around Lewis" we kept looking and waiting in our defensive hedgehog. In quick succession torches one after the other began lighting up attached to stone walls until we were enclosed in a huge ring of fire, then the chanting and stomping of feet begun once again. Appearing like ghostly apparitions, the seats and walls of a great arena began to take form and the torches shot up the stands. The cheering was thousands of ghostly figures sitting on stone seating, chanting and applauding filling the room with noise and anticipation. Looking around the arena we stood in our spot looking at a huge metal gate that loomed on one side with a great metal bar and chains lashed across it. In the stands the stone seating was shadowed by great stone arches that ran the length of the ridge. The wall down into the pit we were standing in stood 15ft tall with torches set all around

"it looks like the Colosseum" said Chloe who began examining her surroundings more closely, I tried to focus on the apparitions chanting. The figures had normal bodies but the heads, they didn't seem normal almost canine in form. Simon joked as always

"I don't suppose we can buy seats for this, I'm feeling a little too close to the action" James took his pack off and put it on the ground "everyone, put everything but your weapons on the ground. Be ready for a fight." We did just that pilling our packs together and getting into a circle, those who used shields were spread out trying to give as much cover as possible. The chanting grew louder until it became loud enough for everyone to hear

"SUETEKH, SUETEKH, SUETEKH" their chant filled the great chamber

"don't suppose anyone has google translate to hand do they" said Simon still trying to sound jovial, James turned to Chloe

"you don't have any idea what they are chanting do you?" Chloe looked back

"sorry I have no idea, could be a name, could be a creature" she paused for a second "could be a challenge". Trumpets began to sound, great blasts announcing the beginning of something brilliant, or terrible. In the centre of one of the stands what looked like a small tornado spun round and dispersed to reveal a huge figure with the head of a Jackal "Its Anubis!" shouted Chloe. The figure put its arms out and its voice echoed all around, it began shouting to the crowd who became lively at his words

"oh that can't be good, anyone any ideas?" Simon asked not expecting an answer,

"what is an Egyptian god doing with Roman colosseum?" I asked trying not to sound stupid "I don't think the time line is what's important here mate" Simon answered. Once Anubis stopped talking he turned and looked at us then waved his hand at the metal door. The sound of chains moving, the bar being lifted and then great heavy metal gates being opened began to sound in the chamber. The crowd cheered louder and louder as they heard the screech of the chains and the huge bolt moving. The anticipation was welling up inside, I gripped my sword tightly until my knuckles blushed white waiting to see what would come out. I looked at Lewis who was brandishing his dagger eagerly awaiting the threat. Anubis shouted once more " 'ana 'uetik 'amiat" Arwa swore under her breath and I looked at her as she spoke

"AMMIT, I've read about it, it's a Chimera, one of the worst controlled by Anubis alone, when the scales of justice decided a soul was not worthy the souls heart was fed to Ammit" As she stopped talking a large creature burst out the door with the scaly head of a crocodile, the fore limbs and mane of a lion and the enormous hind limbs of a hippo. It emerged from its den snarling and revelling in the noise of the crowd.

The creature growled loudly causing the crowd to cheer even more, it then began jumping causing the ground to shake and red flames swayed and illuminated the edge of the stadium. It snarled once more and reare up on its back legs, before landing with a thump and began to charge forward

"EVERYONE SCATTER!" it hurtled towards us teeth bore, causing us to split off. Its speed was incredible, James called over "Ryan try to climb into the stands with Lewis the rest of us will flank and get its attention" I picked up Lewis and began running to the wall, as I did I spotted Private Daniels also running towards one of the stands throwing his shield to the ground. The creature charged again not at those holding their weapons or even Lewis and I, but at the soldier fleeing. I didn't stop, I couldn't stop, and my mission was Lewis. Arrows began being hurtled at the creature but just bounced off its thick hide, I reached the wall and just as I did the creature caught up to Daniels. First it smashed him with its massive lions paw throwing him the ground hard, and then grabbed his leg flung him in the air and in one swift motion, he was gone.

"NO!" I shouldn't have shouted I knew I shouldn't. It looked at me dead in the eyes far from satisfied with its first meal "Lewis I need you to crouch down don't move don't make any sound" It reared up again and began its charge once more, I ran faster than I had ever ran before away from the wall and Lewis, but it was no use it started to catch up on me. Just as it was about to turn its head to the side and clamp its jaw on me I dug my sword in the ground using it as an anchor and then pushing myself just under the creatures jaws below its torso, narrowly avoiding its crushing bite. The Creature Ammit tried to see where I had gone causing it to trip and flop over, this giving me precious seconds to regroup with the others, Looking towards the wall I saw Chloe and Arwa trying to get Lewis up into the stands but even between two of them they couldn't, it was as though the wall got taller with every attempt. I got to James "you got a plan?" he looked at me "not a good one, nothing seems to go through the hide even my sword only gave it a shave when it came past first time, If there's a soft spot it's on the inside. Steven try and aim for the eyes, blind it if you can. We have 5 flares left between us, use them to throw the creature off if you can" Looking around I had an idea

"THE SHIELD" James looked at the shield then at me confused "remember the light tricks we use to do, we can toy with it like we did with the neighbour's cat. Maybe the lion part will take the bait" James looked at the shield in the distance not convinced but happy for any ideas "go on but don't do anything stupid, everyone else strike where you can. If it opens its mouth, fire what you can inside" Splitting off into groups of three and not a second too soon as the creature was already rearing up to charge again, we each try to distract dodge and strike, but the creature didn't want to open its mouth too often almost as though it knew our plan. Twice I got its attention reflecting light from the torches and tried to get it, but it moved too quickly for me to get anything in or near its mouth. Just as James was trying again the creature turned and spotted Lewis, Chloe and Arwa. Looking almost gleeful at the easy prey it started running towards them as they continued to try and scramble Lewis up the wall. Charging faster and faster with hungry intent, it opened its mouth wide, Lewis had just grabbed the ledge of the wall when Arwa lit a flare and as the dazzling blaze blinded the creature she then dove out of the way, causing it to crash into the wall. My heart sank as everything disappeared in a cloud of dust that had been kicked up in a great plume of powdered rubble hewn red by the flare. We were all running towards it when the dust began to clear and debris lay all around, but I could no longer see Lewis's hands on the wall and I froze

"HELP!" Chloe's and Lewis's voices erupted from the dust and the Chimera came running from the wall bucking up and down erratically. I looked closely only to see my little brother and Chloe holding on for dear life on the lions mane. I didn't give it a second thought, I starting running towards the Chimera sword in hand as it kept bucking and I saw as Chloe and Lewis gripped as hard as they could. I lunged forward with both hands bringing my sword down aiming at its elongated mouth, as my arms felt the sword make contact with the creature's snout it felt as though there was nothing stopping my blade cutting through and my arms dropped to the ground holding tightly to the hilt. I looked at my sword, only a fraction of the blade remained. Staring at what was left I then looked at where the remainder rested, cutting through to bone my blade lay dug in the snout of the creature held like a stick in sand dripping blood down the broken blade. I felt its eyes digging through me as it forgot about the two on top and focused only on me, it opened its jaw once again to snap me up and I threw myself to the floor rolling between its legs. I rolled under it narrowly missing its lion claws and huge hippo feet from shredding or trampling me and it kept looking for where I had went. I could hear James shouting in the distances as I continued to roll around narrowly dodging every step. Rolling out behind the creature I saw it trying to claw the shard from its snout with its paw, I looked at James who was getting the others to surround it holding their weapons up, the creature still in pain began to rear up trying to swipe at them, I could see Mia trying to get centre with it while James moved to the back

"NOW" James shouted and everyone took two steps forward the Chimera reared up high once again thrashing its claws. James pirouetted and landed a heavy swipe at the Achilles tendons of the creature's great hippo legs, breaking the skin causing it to drop to down. As it came crashing down it let out a painful howl, it dropped its head down looking for its quarry. A short cry and then everything fell silent as the creature slid down Mia's spear. As it dropped I saw that the tip pultruded from the creatures skull where Lewis and Chloe were. As the creature had reared then dropped she had dug her spear in the ground where it would impact using the creatures own power against it. It continued to slide down then drop with a thud "you two ok" James called out. Lewis slid down from the creatures back and said worriedly "Chloe's hurt" we went to the other side of the creature where Chloe was still holding on to the mane, as the spear tip had pierced the creature skull It had also pierced her arm smashing her gauntlet and dripping blood everywhere, squinting painfully she shouted

"look I'm happy its dead and all but this fucking hurts!" Mia ran over unscrewed the point then pulled Chloe arms off and examined the wound "its ok its missed your artery's, but your gauntlet is beyond, well its fucked" Arwa re-joined us and quickly clotted the wound, she wrapped a bandage around Chloe's arm and put it in a makeshift sling. We had forgotten entirely that we were being watched.

Anubis began shouting but we still couldn't understand anything he shouted, that was until everything that was once sitting down began to stand

"I don't think the tournaments over guys" Simon took two daggers out and we watched as they began to jump down from the stands. What was once just distant figures were now tall creatures with the heads of jackals and carrying weapons and blood lust. James held up his sword

"form a perimeter, Chloe and Lewis stay close to the Chimera" Anubis roared so loudly it echoed everywhere and the Jackals began charging towards us bearing their teeth for the attack. I grabbed the shield from the ground that I had been using and Chloe threw me her sword with her good arm, watching them run towards us I stood firm I was not about to be beaten not now that we were so close. The first leapt up to slash me with its sword, using James's technique I pirouetted and using the base of the shield I smashed its sword aside then thrust my sword through its neck watching it turn to dust and ash. The second came running forward, I parried its attack and it kept lunging forward. Block, block, parry, jab and smash with shield cut the head, dust and next foe. There must have been 50 to 60 plus that kept coming at us but we did not flinch, this journey had already cost us so much, it will not cost us anymore. In a flurry of acrobatics and sword play James and I unleashed fury upon our attackers, blocking and breaking their charges then slashing them to ash. Mia and her spear was a blur of red hair and metal, she blocked three attackers then skewered the first, cut the legs from the second, crushed the skull of the third and then dug the tip back in skull of the second. Simon and Steven in an array of Ranged and short attacks slew everything that came at them. Arwa and the others did not let down the side; everything that came upon us was cut down as though we had been looking forward the whole journey to a proper fight. More kept coming and in a beautiful display of synchronised sword play James and I had almost made a clearing for ourselves. I crushed the next ones head with the base of the shield then I heard Chloe shout

"RYAN!" I spun around to see Chloe trying desperately to grab the leg of one of the creatures that had grabbed Lewis and leapt round to our flank trying to escape

"STEVEN!"I shouted and Steven spotted strait away. He began shooting arrows at the creature trying to bring it down but the other monsters kept leaping and taking the arrows. I ran at it with all the speed I could muster dodging the swords of the creatures that remained, as I ran across the stadium barely gaining on it, I looked at my shield "this had better work" In my sprint I spun around then launched the shield at the creature, it flew like a discus and smashed into its legs buckling it down. As I caught up the creature lifted its weapon to slash me, but I was already upon it and I swiped my sword cutting its head clean off. Lewis fell and lay in the pit of ash blowing a raspberry of soot. I pick him up out of the ash "are you ok?" I scrambled to see if he had been hurt at all

"I'm ok, thanks" I looked at James and the others who had just cut down the last of the attackers. I then looked at Anubis whose gaze was fixated on Lewis, he let out a roar and I gripped the sword awaiting him to attack next, but the roar did not signal an attack. The wall opposite to the way we came in began to hollow and a bridge formed up giving us passage, as I looked back at Anubis, he was gone and the whole stadium became dim until only the torches leading us out were still lit. James ran over

"you two ok?" I picked Lewis up then matted his hair and held him close

"yeah all good" Lewis and I smiled at each other. The others came up behind and I heard Simon

"I'll say, nice one Steve Rodgers that was a slick move" Simon was walking up behind the others holstering his many knifes and I laughed

"yeah well, it didn't come flying back to me now did it" I shrugged trying to play it off "you ok Chloe?" I saw her coming over with Mia's help and her arm in the splint

"I'll live, sorry that thing came out of nowhere I couldn't grab Lewis in time" I smiled at her

"If you did I'm not going to lie, in your condition I would have been bloody impressed, but with a torn up arm you did everything you could just shouting me gave us everything we needed" Not willing to sheath our weapons we gather our packs and proceeded towards the exit constantly watching over our shoulders.

# Chapter 24

## The Assault Part 2
### (The Fort)

Brian watched the smoke and dust clear on the battlefield when he spotted something in the distance

"what the hell is that?" He focused his eyes on the shadows in the clearing, his eyes then began to widen "BRACE THE GATE!" he shouted. Rolling towards the gate where the huge boulders that were hurled out in the beginning, racing towards the gate they showed every intent on smashing into and destroying the fortifications. Brian took up the 50cal rifle and loaded the explosive rounds, he began firing rounds as quick as his shoulder could handle them. He aimed at the oncoming projectiles, several exploded even as they veered and swerved to avoid his shots. But it wasn't enough, three had committed to the main gate and in a crushing, ear splitting shatter of metal, the gate broke apart throwing soldiers all over and scattering those gathered in the square. Major Campbell shouted

"THEY'RE GOLEMS!" The larger Golem along with its two companions stood upright opening like great stone transformers and then roared. Bullets rained upon them doing very little as they began picking up and crushing those they had blown away from the main gate, Brian tried to aim at one of the creatures eyes just as a small "ting" sounded beside him. He stopped and looked round just as grandad shouted "GRENADE OUT!" it landed directly between the Golems and not second to soon, as they looked at this tiny rock thrown between them curiously and then exploded leaving nothing but sand and rubble. Brian looked up at the hollow gate that was now wide open and saw as everything was now on its way. Brian looked at Popps who once again unsheathing his sword, hell had broken loose and they were all that stood in its path, he whispered under his breath "Chloe I hope you're ok, I…"

# Chapter 25

## Level 9
### The Frozen Lake

Weaving our way down the last passage we began to feel tired and decided to rest a bit before our last trial. I pull a fruit bar out of my pack open it and begin to chew without any thought for its flavour or texture. All I could feel was just that my body needed food of some kind, whatever I had left. Staring off into space I begin to forget where I'm sitting, that the walls and red earth around me stood only feet apart and kept me trapped. Anywhere around me demons could be scrambling in other tunnels to the surface to attack my friends and family

"are you ok?" I shake my head and look right to see Chloe looking at me and I smile

"yeah I'm good, how's your arm?" she gives it a small movement "been better, more pissed about my gauntlet. Scholars are going to chew me out for breaking it" I smile

"wasn't exactly your fault and I think damaged gear will be the least of our worries once we get back up there" I felt myself about to say if we do but pessimism wasn't something I or anyone needed "The LT is never going to trust us again after this, I almost forgot here's your sword" I pick up Chloe's sword holding the hilt towards her, she looks at it

"no use to me at the moment I'll get it off you later" I put the sword back down next to the shield and look to see her mind wander. I know she's thinking of Brian, thinking if he responds she won't know

"he never remembers to check his messages anyway, I wouldn't worry" she smiles and agrees, but I know it's a hollow smile still filled with worry. Steven and Simon are at the back of the group laughing away about their performance in the stadium with the others and Lewis sitting with them, listening to their accounts of the previous chambers. James and Mia are little bit further along the tunnel with Mia attempting to thrust food at James

"Come on babe you've got to eat something keep your strength up" Mia looks at him sternly thrusting it into his hand

"fine, but anymore of these things and I'll need to finish a box of Laxatives just to feel normal again" Mia laughs

"shut the fuck up that's mingin" James takes a bite and chews then Mia puts her arms around him.

I don't know why, I wasn't even sure it was me who did it until I looked at everyone staring at me, angry and zealous I shouted loud

"KNOCK IT OFF YOU TWO THIS IS HARDLY THE PLACE" they and everyone else was now staring at me and I thought it was someone else in the room who shouted, but it was me

"oryt Ryan no need to lose it" James says as Mia takes her arms down. I didn't apologise I was still trying to figure out what happened, as everyone else around me stared. After 10 minutes of silence James rustled everyone then we were all gathering our gear, I looked up at Simon who was looking at me oddly

"you've got to get that temper checked mate, I know you're a bit jealous of James and Mia but you need to keep your shit together down here" he puts his hand out, I grabbed it and hoisting myself up

"I didn't even know it was me?" He look me in the eyes

"we all fucking knew it was you mate" I scrunch my face looking at the ground

"yeah but, I dunno it didn't feel…" I turned away then we set off down the tunnel again. As I walk along with my head bowed bobbing along with my own thoughts, I notice that a lot of moisture begins to form on the walls all around. I reach out my hand, to the touch the walls they feel cold and clammy with damp beginning to fill the air. I'm not the only one that noticed as I see others touching the wall, but my mind was already racing and I gave it very little much thought. Another familiar cool breeze starts to blow past us both cooling and unsettling our nerves. My head was still reeling from what happened at the last stop and I couldn't concentrate. I didn't notice the shards of rock forming above me or the crystal sparkling in the rocks that darted all around. I didn't realise until the frozen mist that was my breath, blew back into my face and I coughed on it. Breathing deep feeling that menthol like blast, I begin to take in my surroundings and all my senses begin to stand on end. As we walk forward we enter another chamber only this time we stand looking over a huge frozen lake. The lake is surrounded by a rocky crystallised shore, ice and stone stalagmites and stalactites decorated the cavern roof and floor. The shards created both a beautiful and terrifying chamber of ominous dwelling, light seemed to be reflecting from somewhere illuminating everything. James unshoulders his pack again

"put down anything you don't need to defend yourself here, it won't help you in this room. Chloe stay close to the entrance I don't want you in this fight" Chloe begrudging but understandably sits next to the packs at the entrance. I began to quiver holding my sword, not because I was cold, I wasn't even afraid. I knew this chamber well, after all, I had seen it before. I had felt the cold air in my lungs. No the shaking wasn't me it was everything else, a pulse was reverberating all round. Walking further in I began to feel drawn to the lake, I was longing for it.

"It's fuckin Baltic in here" exclaimed Mia, James sounded tense still looking around for a path or gate

"shhh" As he look round he spotted me moving forward "Ryan where are you going?" I could hear him and he got louder while trying to be quiet but his wasn't the only voice I could hear. The second voice wasn't even loud, it was barely audible, but my feet kept moving. Forward I marched echoes of voices all around me, until I heard a resounding crunch under foot. The frozen water shore was now under my feet and began to crack, what started as a splinter began to creep like lightening forking through the sky. Each fresh fork created a beautiful glacial ricochet all around the cavern causing the icicles above to quiver. Looking across the lake I stand frozen as the ice begins to bulge and lift "everybody fan out use the rocks for cover RYAN! Get back from there!" My feet weren't moving I was rooted to the ground. Out of the growing tide created by the broken ice, I saw as the water broke, through wash and ripples I watched as something large began to surface. A huge water serpent's head had begun to rise, its massive head like that of a bearded dragon was swaying back and forth as it shook the ice from its blue, grey and green scales before fixating its onyx pupils upon me. Its body rose from the water with a huge eel like tail that lapped the surface and its fork tongue slithered through razor sharp teeth. I knew then this is what had called me to this place, this was the voice in my head all this time. It thrashed the water around breaking the ice until only a crystal blue lake slapped the shore. It seemed to be stretching as though awaking from a deep sleep, but never letting go of its gaze upon me. I could hear everyone around me, but no voice was as clear as the creature before me which began to speak and cloud all other thoughts

"I am the great LEVIATHON and you have releasssed me, you will be rewarded my pet" its head moved almost pointing towards the rocks behind me "you dessserve her, you will be my champion in the war to come, sssslay all of these puppets ssslay them" I felt my ribs being thrust and legs leave the ground. Simon had tackled me once again to the ground and I began to snap out my trance. The serpent began to writhe and thrash as arrows began to be fired at it and it let out a screeching wail which caused the icicles above to drop and creatures of all kinds began to emerge from small tunnels all around. Grabbing Chloe's sword tightly I got to my feet and looked for Lewis who was being held close by James behind a rock

"what the hell was that Ryan?" James looked angry but I didn't answer, I looked back at the serpent that had begun jabbing into the rocks trying to catch Simon and the others. Imps, Demons and hell hounds began rushing towards us, I grabbed the shield and sword and started slashing down everything that came forward. 1 demon, 2 demons, 3 demons one came rushing forward when a huge ice shard came crash down straight from the ceiling on top of it. As I took a second look at the skewered demon, a dog rushed forward and tackled me to the ground. I blocked its jaw with the sword but the strength and force of the dog forced me over, as I crash to the ground I can feel its claws trying to tear me. Failing to cut my armour I kicked the dog over me, rolled over and dig my sword deep. Regaining my feet I look around and hear Lewis shout in fear

"RYAN!" in that instance I noticed he had started glowing brightly and at the back of the room out of the corner of my eye I spotted it. "The gate, it's over there!" James looked where I was pointing and nodded at me acknowledging the route to take. James shouted to the others "Cover us, keep her busy!" the three of us began to weave in and around the rocks, two demons stood swords in hand to cut us off, without missing a beat James and I run them through beckoning Lewis to keep up. As we ran the serpent spotted us, it then spotted Lewis and started thrashing towards us. I grabbed Lewis and took cover behind a rock as the huge figure crushed stone around us searching for him. James grabbed the biggest rock he could and flung it at the leviathan's head causing it to recoil back

"get him to the gate Ryan!" James shouted. Dropping the shield and picking Lewis up I began to run as fast as my legs would take me, the serpent was frantically attacking James who slashed at its head as it dived to snatch him up. I could see the light from the gate up ahead, its phosphorus glare was highlighted against the dismal cavern walls, and we were almost there. More and more creatures came into the cavern attacking everyone from all angles, hacking slashing, biting and gnawing. Armed only with my sword I moved in and about the rocks with Lewis, only stopping to take down any foe that persisted to slow my progress. Picking up Lewis once again we are now so close to the gate I can make out the symbols marked around the archway, I became so focused on my goal I didn't see it coming. The serpent's huge tail rose out of the water and lashed out, I managed to spin just in time to put my back to it as it crashed against us and it hurtled Lewis and I through the air summersaulting barely missing jagged rocks all around us before landing with a thud my head banging off a rock. My head dazed, pounding and ears ringing I could hear myself shouting Lewis as though through a pillow

"where are you Lewis? Are you ok?" Lewis came into sight but blurred

"Ryan come on, come on" I felt his hand on my arm trying to raise me up just like he did each morning with little success. As I got to my knee trying to raise myself a loud clang sounded beside me, I looked right to see James's sword dug into the ground next to me

"look after them little brother they need you" Still dazed I watched as James picked up Lewis and began to sprint towards the gate, he raced over and rushed passed every demon and obstacle in his way. Watching in shock I see the tail once again swinging round but James gracefully leaps over it regains his footing and in one bound hurtles through the shimmering gate. In one singular moment, James and Lewis, were gone. Everything was in slow motion the Leviathan and every creature along with every Pathfinder stood and stared at the gate as it began to shine brighter and brighter. It sounded like a generator building up or an electrical charge getting ready to burst with energy all around, I could feel the radiance pulsing from it as the light shining through got brighter and brighter, the noise is getting louder and louder. The energy climaxed in an almighty burst of light that illuminated the cavern, it sounding like a huge bell being rung. The white shimmer blasted all around the cavern and the shock wave could be felt even heard rising through hell. As it reached each level above the pulse and clang of the hell gates being opened rung like a chorus of bell ringers sounding the Sunday service. The wave swept over me and I witnessed as the demons, imps and hounds blasted into ash upon the pulse. But the Leviathan was not dead, it writhed with agony at the pulsing light as though being hit with a hammer. I looked at my armour, cloak and weapons and watched as white lightning began to jump across the silver symbols. They burned with white flame and I looked at others to see the same across their armour, I shouted instinctively remembering how the light went through my sword into the minotaur

"PUT YOUR WEAPONS IN THE WATER!" everyone lunged at the lake putting their weapons in the water and the lightning flew across striking the leviathan like white spears crossing over, but it wasn't going down. Mia grabbed her spear that was glowing and threw it as hard as she could at the creatures head; the spear flew true and imbedded its phosphorus point in the creature's body. Even through the pain the creature spotted her with a look of vile menace and intent to claim one last victim. It took aim ignoring the light still pulsing over it or the spear hanging from it. Mia was in the open and there was nowhere for her to hide, the Leviathan lunged forward opening its mouth to strike. Grabbing my brother's sword that was imbedded beside me and was now pulsing with unbelievable energy I started sprinting towards Mia. As I ran I lifted the shield I had dropped and sprinted as hard and fast as I could. Mia stood her ground holding her sword with a face of anger, willing to face her death just to strike a deadly blow into the monster and just as the creature was 10ft from her I made contact. Raising my shield arm up I crashed into its head forcing it over, as my right arm buckled with the force of my charge under the shield, my left arm dug my brothers sword deep into the skull of the Leviathan. Narrowly missing Mia, the Leviathan and I rolled over hurtling into the rocks around, as I lost grip on the sword I felt myself going over and under the monster. Rolling to a stop, I land staring into the black eyes of the creature I had now slain watching them glaze over. Though life has left it, I could still feel its gaze upon me burning away before finally a sense of ease came over me, I had been released from her grip and she was dead. I no longer had any strength left and as I heard the others running over to find me, everything went black, my last thought was that of Lewis and James disappearing through the gate

PAUL BENTLEY

# "James, Lewis"

# Chapter 26

### The Stand
**(The Fort)**

The great stampede of hells army loomed before them and every round of ammo left was being fired, but to little avail and now barely slowing anything coming forward. Brian and the other snipers leapt down from what remained of their nests, each grasping sword in hand while some grabbed shields and began joining the rest of the garrison in the square. Major Campbell moved to the front of the line looking at the hoard baring down on them then looking at his sword steeling his nerve he spoke "You are the guardians of the dead" turning now to face the garrison "YOU ARE THE LAST DEFENCE OF THE LIVING" still facing the garrison but now pointing his sword at the growing hoard

"IF HELL IS WHAT THEY WANT" Thinking of his sons his armour began to glow and he thrust his sword in the air "WE. WILL. GIVE. THEM. HEEEEELLLL!!!" Not a single face showed fear as the shout rung all round and war cry's erupted. A fierce determination was emanating all around and the feeling of unconquerable strength gripped each sword, axe, shield and spear. At that moment the first monsters came hurtling through the gate and Dad was the first to rush forward spinning cutting through them like a strimmer through grass. Brian and Popps joined the fight as more and more began pilling through the gate, other creatures began clambering over the walls. Swarming over the fort like a flurry of ants over a sugar cube. More and more pilled in but the garrison showed no leniency to their quarry.

"you oryt lad" Brian spun round to see Popp skewer a demon "I'm running out of floor space here" Popps says then shouts in pain as an imp grasps trying to bite his leg, he punches it with the hilt of his sword and throws it back over the wall "little bastards" a smile breaks on Brain's face and he continues his flurry. Lt Williams came swooping in parrying the attack of a demon smashing it with her axe, she then grabbed one by the neck and pinned it to the wall before breaking it with one hand

"why aren't you in class Brian?" she gives him a stern look then grinned and moves on to the next victim to face her axe

"that's your teacher?!" Popps looks at Brian in amazement "no wonder you lot are tough.

The garrison was being overrun but was not beaten yet, as more creatures emerged, soldiers formed groups to defend one another. Another golem rolled in crashing into a group and without hesitation they dug their swords and spears in immobilising it then striking the killing blow. More furies came swooping down trying to slash and carry soldiers away, as they did Pathfinders dived from the parapets to engage their foes hacking and slashing. As the silver crossed with creature and claw crossed with armour the strain of the battle began to show on weary faces. The Pathfinders were strong and powerful but the opposition was immense in numbers and many began losing. The LT reached Dad

"Major we can't hold this fort much longer they are going to break through any minute.

In the Command centre the loss of soldiers was being reported all over and the Commander looked to the gate at the soldiers that were left to defend it

"Colonel what's going on? Is there anything we can do?" The Colonel conferred with his assistant

"we don't have much left, they are fighting with sword, the only ordinance and reinforcements is what you see at the departures gate, we lose them and we lose our only defence" she tries to think "we lose the fort we have lost already, send them in and arm every cleric and scribe in the office"

"Commander?"

"That's an order". The soldiers at the gate rallied up and awaited the steel wheel moving out of their way. As the alarm sounded and a red light flashed warning of the door opening, the clerics began to assemble in the foyer swapping their clipboards and uniforms for swords and armour. The steel door began to roll then came to a halt and the soldiers began pilling through, the Commander entered the foyer looking at her band of reserves with both fear and pride at the war rally

"you have all received the training and you have all seen the creatures we face, this office must not fall" the clerics and remaining scribes all nodded at this and prepared for battle.

In the fortress the new reserves joined the fight throwing magazines to some and brandishing their swords at the quarry before them. War cries had erupted all around with new purpose and the main square became the focus of the defences. Brian and Popps still holding their ground saw as the new forces helped push back the ever persistent monsters. The battle was far from over and our forces tried to put up defensive positions. The ground began to shake once more and even the creatures took a moment to find its source. The last abomination started to rise from the seal, this time a great hydra with two heads sprung from the ground screeching. Its roar seemed to be causing red fork lightning to strike all around

"Brian get out of the square!" Popps shouted and grabbed Brian by the arm and then started leading him from the square to the battlements but Brian shook his hand off

"we can't leave them" Popps looked back

"we are not out of this fight yet lad trust me" Brian nodded and followed. The creature came crashing into the fortress destroying what was left of the main gate. It began snatching up soldiers all over, as spear and sword tried to hack and slash it but showed no signs of slowing down. Major Williams ran forward trying to rush his sword into its chest but the creature spotted him smashed him with its tail then snatched him up in one gulp, The Lt screamed in fury slashing everything in sight trying to make her way towards the beast. Popps got back to their nest and lifted the 50 cal getting it into position and holding up a large bullet to Brian

"I've got one round left, this one's a special one, it makes armour piercing rounds look like BB pellets, make it count lad" as he loaded it into the rifle he then took his sword out to watch their backs. Brian got down and looked through the sights

"what am aiming for?"

"its heart you muppet, shoot a head and we have an even bigger problem on our hands" Brian looked at it trying to think where a heart would be, grandad thrashed at creatures trying to attack them "hurry up lad these pricks aren't patient" the monster still destroying battlements was not hindered by our forces and as Brian took aim just as one of the heads spotted him and Popps.

On the ground imps once again tried to swarm over spotting that the gate was open, they started flooding again into the office. The Commander stood with her forces pistol in hand "NE OBLIVISCARAS" she yelled as they let loose, shooting and cutting down the creatures that tried to get in. As one leaped over to slash and bite at her it was quickly pinned to the wall by a silver dagger, looking across the room Mum stood in her throwing stance guarding Liam. Mum and the Commander nodded to each other and the Commander continued the fight "protect the souls and protect the living"

Brian seeing the Hydra coming towards him did not look or run away, he focused on aiming at the centre mass of the creature, the round burst from the gun with a mighty crack louder than the crashing thunder, throwing Brian's shoulder back and hurtled into the beast. But nothing happened, the creature startled for a second then lunched at the nest and Popps tackled Brian out of the tower just as the Hydra came crashing in. They fell landing on a pile of wooden boxes covered in cloths that broke upon impact. As the monster lifted its head and rubble fell, Brian and Popps took cover from the fallen rocks looking to see if the Hydra had seen them land.

"What happened to the bullet?" shouted Brian "give it a second lad" grandad shouted, they watched as the creatures chest burst open in a bloody magma and the heads came crashing down "ha what did I tell ya it was a special one" As the beast flopped, Brian could see the gate behind it. An army ten times the size of their current quarry loomed in the distance. A moment of fear gripped Brian, Popps put his hand on Brian's shoulder "lad it's been fun and I'm glad I had you by my side" Brian looked at Popps and shook his hand. Picking up their swords they rose from the boxes and started to charge towards the army coming upon them. Dad, Lt Williams and many others all that had spotted the next threat raised their swords and charged towards the army running towards them. There was nothing they could do but charge and take as many with them as possible. The ground quaked with the running of so many, new strength found those who had been fighting for hours and their war cries provoked fear in hells armies forward line. Just as Brian got to the outside of the great gate he found he was running alongside Popps Dad and Williams they ran with all the strength and will they had left to defend the fort. As the shadow of monsters loomed over them, just as sword was about to crash with demonic flesh a great bell rang all around. It caused everyone and everything to pause looking for where it had come from. It was quickly followed by another 8 rings sounded in quick succession and the monsters that stood before them that were running began to exploded in the pile of ashes. Brian looked back at the fortress and spotted ash was being blown in the wind like a black mist.

In the office the imps that weren't already slew screeched and tried to flee before poof, they were gone in the same black burst of dust . Everyone stood gazing at the gate and each other disbelieving what had just happened. The Commander sword in hand looked at the Great seal on the wall and watched as the ninth gate glowed immensely bright and then was followed by all the other gates which began to shine on once again

"they did it, THEY DID IT, WE HAVE WON" she shouted and a cheer began to erupt across the office even the souls who had been hiding but trying to see what was happening began to cheer. Mum hugged Liam tight, tears pouring down her face

"your brothers are safe they did it".

Out at the fortress Brian, Popps, the Lt and Dad stood together looking at where the seal once lay and then back at the fortress. Dad looking at the Lt put his hand on her shoulder and saw a tear she tried to hide drop down, he raised his sword at the cheers still being bellowed from the fortress. Brian had a thought and started sprinting towards the fortress followed by the others

"why are you running lad?"

"The others they're still down there I need to check the Gauntlet". He got to his bag but it had been crushed by rocks and the gauntlet destroyed. Brian then turned to Dad

"where is yours?"

"I had to give it to Major Williams so he could send his updates" Going towards a soldier Brian took the soldiers rifle, shouldered it and took his spare magazines, he then got a gauntlet off a scribe tending to wounded. Accompanied by two dozen others including Dad and Popps they used ropes to descend into the pit. Lt Williams stayed back to reinforce the garrison, or what was left of it and make sure the office was ok Popps looked at Dad and Brian

"don't worry lads, well find them".

# Chapter 27

## Enlightenment

I awoke tied to a stretcher looking at the rock and stone walls fleeting past me, I tried to move but couldn't

"what? What?" a familiar voice spoke "its ok son we are almost at the surface" the pain across my body was overwhelming and I began to black out again trying to focus on my dad.

Several hours later

Waking up with my head imbedding in a soft feather down pillow, it felt like a dream I was still trying to wake up from. I was no longer in my armour but wearing soft white pyjamas, with a blanket over me. I looked to my left and could see Steven passed out, scratches down his face but a look of peace as he slept. I went to reach for the bottle of water on the side table beside me but as I did the searing pain struck me "ahhh, fuck" Looking at my arm a solid cast was moulded around it and a drip was being fed into the other

"stop Ryan it's broken you shouldn't try to move it and be careful your leg isn't much better" Chloe was sitting up in the bed opposite me with her arm also in a cast. I looked up and down the room at what remained of our group. Mia was curled up not stirring, her red hair flowing over her blanket. Simon and the others were talking away a few beds down sitting on the edge. He looked over at me giving me a nod and grin.

"James, where is he? Where is Lew..." I swivelled my head around looking for him, my memory of events was slowly returning to me and I slumped into my pillow. Chloe spoke softly "he went through the gate Ryan, he and Lewis both went through. When they did go through it caused a chain reaction that opened all the gates and destroyed the creatures all the way up to the surface, they saved us all" Simon walked over and spoke

"and you saved us mate, that shot at the Serpent was mental I thought we were done for when it wasn't going down, especially Mia, then you tackled it and disappeared underneath it". I was staring at my bed covers thinking about everything that happened forgetting they were all there staring at me, the room fell silent and I turned over slowly trying to pull the covers over me, no one believed I was sleeping but they didn't disturb me.

Later my mum, dad and grandad all came to the infirmary, mum had clearly not long heard about what happened to James but tried to smile when she saw me. Everyone including myself, tried to console her with stories of bravery and valiant deeds from both of them. I said how James led us through the trials and Lewis saved me from the Minotaur, but two sons had been taken from her and no amount of pride could make her feel better. She held Liam close as they left and my guilt over not being the one through the gate when I was supposed to be the one looking after Lewis, began to take over me. The tears I held back while talking to everyone, thinking of my brothers made me feel swollen and broken for not wanting to show them.

Three days passed in the infirmary, most had left leaving Chloe and me to recover. The main visitor was Brian who finally said how he felt to Chloe, it was a sweet moment and I don't think they really believed I was asleep when it happened but I didn't want to ruin it for them. She left with him later that day giving me a hug, saying thank you and goodbye. Another two days later, late in the afternoon the Commander's messenger came into the infirmary

"Sargent Campbell, the Commander wishes to know if you have strength enough for a meeting?" I nodded and got out of the bed but with my leg still hurting, he had to help me into a wheel chair, I strained as my am was also still in agony. The messenger then wheeled me through to the commanders office through the main hall. Once in the room I saw Dad and Chloe sitting waiting for me

"hey son"

"hi Ryan" I smiled at them then looked at the Commander

"how are you Ryan?" I gave a small motion towards my arm

"I've seen better days Sir but I'll live" she smiled and the officer pushed me up to the table then left the room. The Commander smiled at me and put her hands on the desk

"Right, now this isn't usual protocol but given recent events I feel the more each of us know the better and we might be able to piece everything together" I looked at dad and Chloe who had clearly already been discussing events already. The Commander put her hands together "a number of years ago a group of Office staff went into hell on their own mission, it failed miserably. Only two were recovered and the souls were lost. Their names were Cleric Robert Jenkins and Cleric Cynthia Hunter. We caught Cynthia after the ceremony and just before the lock down, she was trying to escape into king cross underground in London. We took her to the detention cells where she was not co-operative for hours. That was until the gates were re-opened by your team and from then we couldn't shut her up. It was as though she had just woken up from a long sleep and began to tell us everything she knew" The Commander looked directly at me "your group told me how as you got closer to the ninth gate you began to act, out of character shall we say" I bowed my head, some of my last moments with James where shouting at him for getting close to Mia and the guilt began to flow through me once again, sensing my shame she continued "well, that was because you were being what we call, enthralled" I looked her in the eye and she saw my confusion "it means that your thoughts and actions weren't necessarily your own" She then gestures to Chloe "after some research by Chloe we have figured out the Leviathan is the Demon princess known as Envy one of the seven deadly sins, it is said each human is susceptible to at least one of the deadly sins. The Clerics that went into hell were all enthralled by envy and grew jealous of the Pathfinders. They were looking

159

to prove themselves just as brave and capable as them, they were led straight into her trap. When we sent soldiers to find them and they were retrieved we thought they were saved, but in truth they weren't. When Cynthia was released from the enthral she told us how she and Jenkins were charged to find the Horn of Gabriel, taint it, then take it through the purity gate triggering a spell or failsafe that shut down the gates. The horn is a powerful artefact from one of our founder Pathfinders and research suggests the horn was directly linked with the ninth level of hell. That's why Envy knew what to do with it, how to taint it, but it also explains why it was the only gate not closed. More importantly right now, that's why you acted the way you did Ryan. She was trying to put you under the same spell, you would be a little more resilient being a Pathfinder which is why it took a lot for you to act out. Master Marcus before his death had written that he had been getting visions over the last few years of the cavern you entered, I wanted to ask if you had any visions of the sort?" I nodded my head, I didn't know what to say I should have discussed this more when it was happening instead of ignoring it. I thought about all this and it didn't alleviate any of my guilt. It did explain why my thoughts didn't stay in my head and why I could hear her voice louder as we got closer. The Commander continued her explanation of events "Cynthia got Robert the armour, the clearance to enter hell and opened the door for him to enter purgatory. Robert had spent years trying to find the Horn of Gabriel; we found all sorts of spells drawings, travel documents and research pointing towards it at his house. When he found it, they hatched their plan to get past during the graduation when our guard was lowered for the ceremony. Once he had the horn he performed some kind of spell to taint it, the blast that killed everyone in the cathedral was the tainted horn being blown" I looked at Dad and Chloe who had been taking in the information and Chloe spoke up

"the Horn of Gabriel when blown is supposed to create a great darkness according to prophecy and scripture anyway, it took some interpretation but in this case we guessed it just meant blowing out their eyeballs creating darkness" The Commander nodded at Chloe and spoke again

"Chloe has been instrumental in filling in a number of the blanks in our understanding and we believe that if Envy is tied with the ninth gate then the other sins may also have references that we might un cover" I look at the Commander

"sorry the other sins?" She grips her hands and looks gravely

"we haven't had much information from the citadel, who are currently still carrying out their own investigations, but we reckon this was all tied in with a spell to break out the Princes of Hell from the oldest prison we have records of, Tartarus. The Princes are also known as the 7 deadly sins envy, lust, wrath, pride, sloth, gluttony and greed. Chloe has been doing some research after the information she gathered on your adventure and thrown up some theories on their identities in world cultures. The citadel is investigating the massacres of a handful of Offices around the world. The few survivors left have given accounts of demons being led by formidable leaders but that's all the information we have on them just now. Chloe in the next few months, once she has fully recovered, is going to be going to the citadel as a scholar on my orders to carry on her research and maybe provide us with some intelligence from the citadel if possible. The citadel under the circumstances is currently ignoring our information, despite your actions and accounts." Questions were reeling through my mind but the first thing I said that came through clear was

"why did hell look like it did, you know the way Dante wrote it? And how did you find us?" Dad was the one to answer

"with the information from your accounts we suspect that he found ancient records from when the princes were in power, we think Dante did embellish the story with his own thoughts to make the poem but it seems to follow your adventure fairly closely, beyond that a lucky guess. As for finding you after the gates were opened hell went back to normal just a labyrinth of tunnels, Brian grabbed another gauntlet to track your team, we were with you about an hour after the blast" Chloe beamed at hearing Brian use the gauntlet.

The Commander didn't seem to want anything else discussed just now

"It's time we adjourn this meeting, Ryan we will be holding a ceremony next week to commemorate those we have lost and congratulate your group for their heroism. Ryan I know it might be tough but we thought you might want to say something for your brothers at the ceremony" I considered this

"what would I say?" Chloe put her hand on my shoulder

"you are both heroes, you and your brother. He would have wanted you to be the one who said something" I was going to argue but simply nodded

The Commander continued

"Ryan there is going to be many others wanting to give you their prayers and thanks for what has happened. For that reason you are going on leave same as the others until you are healed and we have managed to rebuild the fortress, it could be a couple of months" the Commander stood up "Ryan I want to take this moment to give you my thanks without you lot none of us would be here. Should you wish to talk, my office is always open" we left the office and dad began wheeling me to the car. As we passed through the hall I looked at the seal on the wall with the light glowing and thought to myself I'm sure it used to be brighter. As Dad wheeled me out he slowed down a bit

"Ryan did anyone mention the glowing to you?" I tried to look up at him

"what glowing?"

"Well when we found you, you were still glowing, you know when you charged up before killing envy. You didn't stop until we reached the surface, we could even feel the aura off you" I tried to imagine how I looked on the stretcher

"no one said anything" Dad gave a slight

"huh" and we got in the car. We didn't talk much on the way home and I went straight to my bedroom when we got there.

# Chapter 28

## *Ceremonies and Eulogies*

I then spent the next week thinking about what to say at the ceremony, but whenever I thought about James and Lewis I could only remember the last moments as James dug the sword into the ground next to me. Then watching them rushing towards the gate, leaping through and just disappearing followed by a bright ray of light. One minute my brothers were with me, I could see them, hear them, hold them and then the next. They were gone and I didn't say goodbye, I couldn't even bury James. Holding my pen sitting at my desk this time I could feel the tears fall down my face and land on the blank paper. It was the first time I had really cried since the realisation that they were truly gone and it felt good. Looking around my room I was reminded of the moments in my childhood when we would play together and torment our parents. Looking at my bed I thought of Lewis waking me up in the mornings to go to school and I smiled thinking of his bravery throughout hell. He didn't cry, he was never scared, he trusted me and believed in me. Wiping the tears from my face I turned back to the piece of paper and began to write.

The day of the ceremony I went outside to get into the car with mum and dad to go to the office, as I stepped outside I looked over and dad walked towards me. Here you go son, he held out his hand and handed me a set of keys "he would have wanted you to have it, but look after it, you know how annoyed he'll be if you don't" it was the keys to James's prized beetle, he had worked nearly his whole life on this car. Clutching the keys I thanked Dad, hugged him and walked to the garage where the car sat dormant. I sat in the driver's seat and looked up; swinging from the mirror was a pyramid picture frame spinning round. The first image was Lewis and Liam on Christmas day getting excited over a large box labelled for them, the second was mum and dad on one of our family holidays standing on a stone bridge and the third was James and I covered in mud in camouflage clothing after our birthday paintball outing at the age of 10. His arm was over my shoulder as we had won the capture the flag challenge. I looked at the smiles staring at me without a care in the world and I pulled back a tear. I started the engine and set off for the Office grinning remembering all our happy memories.

The Ceremony went as expected; a representative from the Citadel Council had come to present our group with medals. Others from the garrison and the Office for their acts during the raid also received medals including Brian, for expert marksmanship and Popps for answering the call to arms despite retirement. Dad stood up to receive James's medal and I heard mum whimper as he did so.

After the presentation he gave a speech thanking everyone for their actions and giving special mention to those who lost their lives defending both the fortress and the office. A number of people stood up giving their eulogies for family members they had lost. We didn't give full details of how some of our companions died only that it was quick and valiant. Before long it was my turn, the Councillor announces me and I approach slowly, holding my crumpled notes. As I reached the podium I then looked out into the crowd.

My throat felt dry but I was determined to give my speech, giving a cough to clear my throat I begin "Everyone has probably heard stories or rumours of what happened in hell. I can tell you that I lost some good friends and loved family. They gave their lives to save everyone and neither I nor anyone else can ever repay them for that. We saw things in hell that no amount of training can ever prepare you for, but we completed our mission and I believe they know their sacrifices were not in vain. My brother James in no small measure was how we made it through to the end. He beat himself up worst of all for those he couldn't save, but still he pressed on because he knew that not carrying on would insult their memory. He led us through parts of hell that could destroy the spirit of the most experienced of soldiers and no matter how blind he was to what was coming, he made us believe that we could push through. He saw our best talents and made sure that we looked after one another, he was a great leader and a great brother. In our darkest spots I didn't show his strength, but he didn't scorn me or cut me off. He got me to stand up and do my job, never losing faith that I could do it" I paused for a second feeling one tear on my cheek, I wiped it away quickly then carried on "My little brother Lewis was a little champion, he never showed fear no matter the dangers that lay ahead and he gave us all the strength to see the mission through. He is the smallest and greatest hero I will ever know and I know that when he passed through that gate, he was never afraid. Thank you all for your wishes" I looked at Liam cuddled into mum and stepped down from the podium. I wasn't sure if I was really done, but I knew I couldn't finish another word standing there. Even though I felt like there was so much more I could have said there wasn't time for it. Today was to say thank you for what they had done. I will have time enough to remember them both, I went over to mum and dad hugged them then hugged Liam who also hadn't shed a tear despite missing his brother.

As the afternoon came to a close and I had spoken to people families, I grouped up with my friends. This was the first time we had all been together again since the infirmary. As I spoke to them they stopped talking and I turned round to see Mia walking towards me carrying something "James would have loved that" I could see where the tears has been running down her face and I tried to smile

"thank you" she lifted the item in her hand and I realised, it was his sword. I looked her in the eyes, her beautiful glistening blood shot eyes "he would have wanted you to have it Mia" she shook her head

"I don't do swords it'll only gather dust, he wouldn't want it to be that way. Besides, your sword is broken and no-one could make one better than him" I smiled at this comment and took it by the hilt, un-sheathed it and looked at the carefully engraved beetle and smiled even more

"thank you". I hugged people, shook hands and then the day was over it was time to move on.

# Chapter 29

## *Beer*

As we all dispersed from the office to our own towns, most of us from Brathaidh decided to go and stay in the pub to raise a toast or drown our tears. As I sat at the table I stared at my pint glass watching the froth bubble away on the amber liquid in front of me "hey man you ok?" I looked up to see Simon taking a large swig then holding his glass and looking at me. The others came and sat down on the pew and began pulling over wooden chairs. Grandad was standing at the bar debating with Brian who got the most amounts of kills and eventually settled with them both buying three rounds of rusty nail shots.

"I know you don't need everyone telling you what he would have wanted, but if there was one thing your brother wanted. It was to you to enjoy your pint" I smiled thinking of nights out in the pub singing songs Simon continued "and what he would have wanted was us all to sing his favourite drinking song" Simon stood up and began to encourage the whole bar to start singing which they did reluctantly to begin with, but eventually erupted in laughter and chorus as the house band joined in. As he reached the part of the song where Charlie stands at heavens gates, I think of James being asked if he did good in his life, then being welcomed into heaven like a hero. At that moment I joined in and the warm feeling of happiness takes hold of everyone tightly. We all become louder and more riotous so much so, that no sooner had the song finished than Simon started it again and we sang louder and happier than ever. No-one would be forgotten, they did not die for nothing. They made their families proud and they will never be forgotten.

## ♪♪ Charlie Mops ♪♪

A long time ago, way back in history,
when all there was to drink was nothin but cups of tea.
Along came a man by the name of Charlie Mops,
and he invented a wonderful drink and he made it out of hops.

HEY

He must have been an admiral a sultan or a king,
and to his praises we shall always sing.
Look what he has done for us he's filled us up with cheer!
Lord bless Charlie Mops, the man who invented beer beer beer
tiddly beer beer beer.

A barrel of malt, a bushel of hops, you stir it around with a stick,

the kind of lubrication to make your engine tick.
40 pints of wallop a day will keep away the quacks.
Its only eight pence hapenny and one and six in tax,

HEY

He must have been an admiral a sultan or a king,
and to his praises we shall always sing.
Look what he has done for us he's filled us up with cheer!
Lord bless Charlie Mops, the man who invented beer beer beer
tiddly beer beer beer.

The Redmans bar, the Lions Pub, the Hole in the Wall as well
one thing you can be sure of, its Charlie's beer they sell
so all ye lads a lasses at eleven O'clock ye stop
for five short seconds, remember Charlie Mops 1, 2, 3, 4, 5.

HEY

He must have been an admiral a sultan or a king,
and to his praises we shall always sing.
Look what he has done for us he's filled us up with cheer!
Lord bless Charlie Mops, the man who invented beer beer beer
tiddly beer beer beer.

On the day that Charlie died he knocked on heaven's gate.
He said to St Peter well tell me how I rate,
Peter looked at him and said well tell me who are you?
He said I'm Charlie Mops and he was sent straight through.

Hey

He must have been an admiral a sultan or a king,
and to his praises we shall always sing.
Look what he has done for us he's filled us up with cheer!
Lord bless Charlie Mops, the man who invented beer

He must have been an admiral a sultan or a king,
and to his praises we shall always sing.
Look what he has done for us he's filled us up with cheer!

Lord bless Charlie Mops, the man who invented beer beer beer
tiddly beer beer beer.

The Lord Bless Charlie Mops.

# Chapter 30

## The plans in motion

Sitting alone in the dark on a rock, smoking a cigarette and looking out into the wilderness of the Nevada desert, a figure sits with mouse blonde hair and bright white pupils. He looks right to see three other figures walking towards him out of the darkness.

"Greetings brothers, it's been a long time coming but we are finally out" the figure on the rock stands up

"too long indeed brother" Another figure walks forward

"they killed our sister and restarted the gates" the first speaks

"a minor setback, she did her job. We are free and if our informant in the citadel is correct they think the danger has passed anyway. It all works to our advantage" the second speaks "you think the ones still below will do their jobs?" the first looks angry at this

"I trust them to know what will happen if they betray us" he walks forward the turns around staring at them all

"you all know where to go and what to do, don't draw attention to yourselves. Not yet anyway" he grins at them and they turn around to walk away.

"The world doesn't know it yet, but the fun, has only just begun"

Printed in Poland
by Amazon Fulfillment
Poland Sp. z o.o., Wrocław

57326920R00101